DEVIL DANGER

My skis left the ground as the mountain
dropped away below me. I was flying.

And there – right where I was going to land! –
crouched a Tasmanian devil.

I don't know who got the bigger fright, me or the devil.
But the animal reacted first. Baring its teeth like a giant black rat,
it spun around to meet me.

You can't change directions when you're airborne. All I could do
was part my legs so my skis landed on either side of the devil.
But not out of range of those fearsome jaws.

Snap!

Puffin Books

www.justindath.com

EXTREME ADVENTURES

DEVIL DANGER

JUSTIN D'ATH

Puffin Books

For Josh, Ben, Charlotte and Dominic

PUFFIN BOOKS

Published by the Penguin Group
Penguin Group (Australia)
250 Camberwell Road, Camberwell, Victoria 3124, Australia
(a division of Pearson Australia Group Pty Ltd)
Penguin Group (USA) Inc.
375 Hudson Street, New York, New York 10014, USA
Penguin Group (Canada)
90 Eglinton Avenue East, Suite 700, Toronto, Canada ON M4P 2Y3
(a division of Pearson Penguin Canada Inc.)
Penguin Books Ltd
80 Strand, London WC2R 0RL, England
Penguin Ireland
25 St Stephen's Green, Dublin 2, Ireland
(a division of Penguin Books Ltd)
Penguin Books India Pvt Ltd
11 Community Centre, Panchsheel Park, New Delhi – 110 017, India
Penguin Group (NZ)
67 Apollo Drive, Rosedale, North Shore 0632, New Zealand
(a division of Pearson New Zealand Ltd)
Penguin Books (South Africa) (Pty) Ltd
24 Sturdee Avenue, Rosebank, Johannesburg 2196, South Africa

Penguin Books Ltd, Registered Offices: 80 Strand, London WC2R 0RL, England

First published by Penguin Group (Australia), 2009

3 5 7 9 10 8 6 4 2

Text copyright © Justin D'Ath, 2009

The moral right of the author has been asserted.

Series design by David Altheim © Penguin Group (Australia)
Cover design by Evi O. © Penguin Group (Australia)
Cover image by Sam Hadley
Typeset in ITC Officina Sans Book by Post Pre-press Group, Brisbane, Queensland
Printed in Australia by McPherson's Printing Group, Maryborough, Victoria

National Library of Australia
Cataloguing-in-Publication data:

D'Ath, Justin.
Devil Danger / Justin D'Ath.

ISBN: 978 0 14 330372 5.

Tasmanian Devils – Juvenile fiction.

A823.3

puffin.com.au

FSC
Mixed Sources
Product group from well-managed
forests and other controlled sources

Cert no. SGS-COC-004121
www.fsc.org
© 1996 Forest Stewardship Council

1
SHISHKEBAB!

I shot over a snowy crest. My skis left the ground as the mountain dropped away below me. I was flying.

And there – right where I was going to land! – crouched a Tasmanian devil.

I don't know who got the bigger fright, me or the devil. But the animal reacted first. Baring its teeth like a giant black rat, it spun around to meet me.

You can't change directions when you're airborne. All I could do was part my legs so my skis landed on either side of the devil. But not out of range of those fearsome jaws.

Snap!

Luckily I was wearing double-layered ski boots. The hard outer shell deflected the devil's razor-sharp teeth. But the impact flicked my right ski sideways. I nearly wiped out. Somehow I stayed upright. Thirty metres past the devil, I slewed to a standstill in a spray of flying snow.

My heart was hammering as I looked back up the slope. I was in Tasmania on Devil's Mountain, but I hadn't expected to *see* one. Weren't they nocturnal? There was a narrow opening under the lip of the ridge. I must have surprised it on its way home.

Then I stopped thinking about Tassie devils, because the sound of voices carried to me on the crisp mountain air. Surprised, I turned to look. I'd thought I had the steep, narrow valley all to myself.

Halfway up the far slope, a pair of white-painted snowmobiles was parked at the base of a pylon. Two men stood beside them. Like their vehicles, the men's ski suits were completely white. No wonder I hadn't noticed them in the snowy landscape. They hadn't noticed me, either, because both men were peering up into the sky.

I looked up, too.

High overhead, a solitary cable car inched across the valley. I watched its slow progress. Something didn't seem right. Even though there wasn't a breath of wind, the big, suspended car bounced and swayed on its cable.

Suddenly there was a thump from the cable car. Its door burst open and I heard a muffled cry.

For a frozen half-second, I saw a young woman's face framed in the doorway. She seemed vaguely familiar. But there wasn't time to think about where I'd seen her before. Too much was going on. Hands were madly trying to stop something from rolling out through the cable car's open door. They were too slow.

The woman screamed, a long, loud wail of despair, as a small doll-like shape plummeted out of the sky.

My heart did a double whammy.

Shishkebab!

It wasn't a doll – it was a baby!

2
WIPE-OUT

The baby dropped like a stone. It didn't make a sound. All I could hear was the hiss of my skis.

The instant the baby fell, I'd launched myself down the mountain with a double pole push.

I was wearing my slalom skis. They're shorter and more manoeuvrable than downhill skis, but not as fast. The terrain worked in my favour. The secluded valley where I'd come to practise for tomorrow's skiing competition was on the western face of Devil's Mountain. The late morning sun hadn't touched it yet. There was still a crust of slippery ice on the snow's surface. Perfect for building up speed.

I crouched into a tuck – knees bent, head down, arms pressed close against my sides – and went for it.

In perfect conditions, and wearing racing skis, an experienced ski-racer can reach speeds of over a hundred-and-forty kilometres per hour. That's faster than the speed limit on any road in Australia.

If there was a speed limit on ski slopes, I probably would have broken it.

I reckon I was going over a hundred when I reached the falling baby. It was going about two hundred.

Luckily both of us were travelling in more or less the same direction. Down. The baby was going straight down, and I was going down at a forty-five-degree angle. So the impact, when we came together, wasn't as bad as it might have been.

WHOMP!

The baby hit my chest like a big, soft football. I let go of my ski poles and grabbed it.

Gotcha!

But we weren't out of trouble yet. I was schussing down the steepest part of the valley, faster than I'd ever skied before. With a baby in my arms!

And there were trees ahead.

I was going too fast to stop before I reached them. It was too late to turn. I only had one option – to sit down.

It must have looked spectacular. From the point where I sat down to the point where I finally stopped somersaulting was roughly fifty metres. I don't remember much of it. All I remember is curling myself into a ball around the baby as I tumbled down the mountain like a human snowball.

I ended up sprawled chest-down in the deep snow between the ice-flecked trunks of two trees. I'd lost my skis and my goggles, and my right sleeve was filled with snow all the way up to the elbow. But nothing was hurting. I seemed to be okay.

What about the baby? asked a little voice in my head.

My hands and arms were empty.

Pushing myself up onto my knees, I blinked down at the sprawling human shape stamped into the snow by my body. The baby wasn't under me. Thank goodness.

So where was it?

I didn't want to go out looking. I was too scared of

what I might find. Nobody that small, that helpless, could have survived such a massive wipe-out.

Then I heard something behind me – a faint mewing cry, like a newborn kitten. I lurched to my feet and fought my way uphill in my big, clumsy ski boots.

The baby lay half buried in the snow just above the tree-line. Its red quilted jacket had turned inside-out, covering its head and face. As soon as I pulled the jacket down, the baby screwed its eyes tightly closed, opened its mouth into a big, wide O, and howled.

The baby's cry brought an instant response.

'TOMMEEEE!' screamed a woman's voice.

I looked up and saw that the cable car had stopped. Two men in blue uniforms were clambering out onto the pylon. Behind them, the woman was hanging out of the cable car's door, her tear-streaked face turned in my direction.

'TOMMEEEE!' she screamed again.

I picked Tommy up. He was pretty upset, bellowing his little lungs out, but he didn't seem hurt.

'HE'S OKAY,' I yelled.

'PLEASE DON'T TAKE HIM AWAY!' the woman cried.

What was she talking about?

'OF COURSE I WON'T TAKE HIM AWAY,' I yelled back.

The young woman brushed the hair off her face and suddenly I remembered where I'd seen her before. On TV. In the newspapers. On the covers of magazines.

It was Princess Monica. The magazines called her *Australia's Princess* – even though she no longer lived in Australia. She was just an ordinary girl from Tasmania, until she met Prince Nicklaus when he was over here on a skiing holiday. They fell in love and got married. Now they lived in a huge palace on the other side of the world. But they'd returned to Australia for a holiday so Prince Nicklaus could compete in the famous Devil's Run Skiing Championships in Tasmania. I'd read all about it in the competition program. In two days' time, provided we both got through our heats, I'd be racing against Prince Nicklaus in the final.

'AREN'T YOU ONE OF THEM?' Princess Monica cried, looking back at me and pointing at the two uniformed men climbing down the pylon.

She wasn't making any sense. But before I could ask what she meant, one of the snowmobiles roared into life.

The other two men – the ones in white ski suits – had jumped onto it. They came flying down the white slope towards me.

Princess Monica was calling out to me again, but the combination of Tommy's crying and the roar of the approaching snowmobile was too loud. For a couple of seconds I puzzled over what she'd said: *Aren't you one of them?*

One of who? I wondered.

I looked down at the small crying baby cradled in my arms. And realised I'd seen him before, too. On TV. In the newspapers. On the covers of magazines. He was Prince Nicklaus and Princess Monica's baby boy, four-month-old Crown Prince Thomas.

I was holding a prince!

Then I remembered the other strange thing Princess Monica had yelled at me: *Please don't take him away.* Suddenly everything made sense.

The two men in blue uniforms were kidnappers! They had dressed up as guards so they could get into the cable car with Princess Monica and kidnap the baby prince. But something went wrong. Princess Monica must have tried to resist them. In the struggle, Prince Thomas fell out of the cable car.

Luckily, I'd been there to catch him.

The snowmobile raced down the slope towards me. Lying in its path was one of my skis. The driver would have seen it, but he drove straight over the top.

It was a two hundred dollar ski!

Shishkebab! The men in white were kidnappers, too! They'd been waiting at the pylon with two camouflaged snowmobiles so all four gang members could make their getaway with the kidnapped prince.

It was too late to run. The snowmobile slid to a stop just up the hill and the driver jumped off. He came wading through the knee-deep snow towards me.

'Give me the baby,' he said.

3
DEEP TROUBLE

Sometimes you act without considering the odds. They were stacked heavily against me. Four men against one fourteen-year-old boy.

But I couldn't let them get the baby prince.

I spun around and headed for the trees.

'LOOK OUT!' yelled Princess Monica.

I glanced over my shoulder. My pursuer had thrown himself flat on the snow and was sledding down the slope on his chest like a giant penguin. It was a smart idea. He could move much faster like that. But it left him wide open to a counterattack. I waited until he was close, then sidestepped and kicked a spray of snow into his face. For a second the sliding man couldn't see where he was going. He shot past me and slammed head-first into a clump of saplings. *Crunch!* A pile of snow fell out of the branches, burying him.

Now was my chance. Hugging the crying baby to my chest, I made a break for it.

'*STOP RIGHT THERE!*' shrieked Princess Monica.

At least I *thought* it was the princess, until I turned around.

The snowmobile's passenger had removed her ski mask and goggles. It was a woman. She was pointing a small black pistol at me.

'Bring me the baby!' she called down through the trees.

Here's what went through my mind at that moment: There was only one reason why anyone would want to kidnap Prince Thomas – ransom. And the ransom for a crown prince would be huge. Millions of dollars.

But the kidnappers would get absolutely nothing if he was dead.

So they wouldn't risk shooting at me when I had Prince Thomas in my arms. I hoped.

Heart in my mouth, I ducked behind the nearest tree.

My gamble paid off – the woman didn't shoot. Her companion was digging himself out of the snow, wheezing and cursing. He was a small man, hardly bigger than me, but he had a pistol too.

Keeping the tree's lower branches between me and the kidnappers, I went ploughing down into the snowy forest as fast as I dared. Which wasn't very fast. I was wearing ski boots. They aren't made for running. And I couldn't risk falling and hurting Tommy.

He'd started crying in earnest now: *Waah waah waah waaaaaah!* He sounded really upset. But there was nothing I could do about it. I had to keep going.

'Shhhh, little guy!' I whispered down at Tommy's small, scrunched-up face. 'They'll hear you.'

But it made no difference whether we were noisy or not. Behind us, my boot tracks went zigzagging through the trees like the trail left by an elephant. A blind man could follow it.

But could a snowmobile?

The trees were getting very close together. I wondered if the kidnappers would be able to manouevre their bulky snowmobile through the maze.

I soon found out. From further up the valley came the whine of a two-stroke engine. It grew steadily louder. Soon it was nearly as loud as Tommy's wailing.

Looking over my shoulder, I glimpsed two white-clad human figures on a white snowmobile dodging through the trees.

'We've got company,' I muttered.

A massive snow-capped boulder loomed above the treetops ahead. It was bigger than a house. Surrounding it was a tangle of bent-limbed snow gums, chest-high saplings and leafy bushes, all powdered with snow. A perfect hiding place. I lumbered towards it, sweating inside my heavy ski clothing. My breath made white clouds around my face. The snow dragged at my boots. Was I going to make it? The sound of the approaching two-stroke engine grew louder and louder. At any moment, I expected to hear a shout behind me.

Or, worse, a gunshot.

But nobody called out. Nobody shot at me. I made it to the bushes. Shielding Tommy with my arms, I put my head down and bulldozed through the leafy tangle. Luckily I was still wearing my ski helmet; it protected my head from the scratchy branches. My Gore-Tex ski suit covered my arms, my body and my legs. I burst out the other side and nearly collided with a wall of damp, black rock.

If I could have kept right on going and magically entered the rock, that's what I would have done. The tangled undergrowth might stop a snowmobile, but it wouldn't stop the kidnappers. It would just slow them down.

I crouched in the snow next to the boulder and tried to catch my breath. The sound of the snowmobile grew steadily louder. And the louder it became, the harder Tommy cried.

'Shhhh!' I said softly.

He was probably cold. I should have thought of that before. Even royal baby clothes aren't designed for going out in the snow for too long. Unzipping the front of my ski suit, I slipped Tommy inside my jumper like a baby kangaroo in its mother's pouch. I pulled the zip back up so just his head was showing.

'Is that better?' I whispered.

Tommy hiccupped, then started crying again. I had

15

to do something or the kidnappers would hear him. They were getting really close.

Maybe he was hungry? I couldn't do much about that. But I remembered what Aunty Erin did once when Nissa, my little cousin, was a baby. They were over at our place and Aunty Erin had forgotten to bring Nissa's dummy, so she let Nissa suck on her fingertip.

I whipped off one glove and offered Tommy a finger. He latched on like it was a dummy and started sucking. It stopped him crying in the nick of time.

The snowmobile came to a standstill on the other side of the bushes. It was only a couple of metres away, but the kidnappers didn't know we were there. I could hear snatches of conversation above the idling engine.

'. . . can't see anything . . .'

'. . . out the other side . . .'

Then the engine revved up and the kidnappers went roaring off around the boulder, looking for the place where my tracks came out of the bushes. But they weren't going to find anything. In thirty seconds, they'd do a complete circuit of the boulder and be back where they started. Then they'd work out what was going on.

Unless I did a disappearing act.

I counted slowly to ten, then gently pulled my finger from Tommy's mouth and bulldozed out through the bushes. Tommy started crying again, but there was nothing I could do. A crying baby is better than a choking baby, which was what might have happened if I tripped over while I had a finger in his mouth. I could hear the snowmobile on the other side of the boulder. I had about fifteen seconds left. I hoped it was long enough. Placing my feet carefully in the boot tracks I'd made coming the other way, I lumbered away from the boulder as fast as I could. I just made it into the trees when I heard the snowmobile come roaring around the side of the boulder. It slowed down and stopped, but the motor kept running.

Would they notice I'd doubled back on my tracks?

Would they hear Tommy? He was crying his little heart out. I bent my thumb so he could suck on the knuckle while I walked. It was too big to choke on and stopped him crying. I heard the snowmobile stop, too. The stutter of its two-stroke engine echoed faintly through the mountains even after it was turned off. Then I heard the kidnappers' voices.

'. . . no other tracks . . .'

'. . . must be still in there . . .'

It had worked! The kidnappers thought Tommy and I were still hiding in the bushes. They'd have to go in on foot to look for us. It would be at least a couple of minutes before they worked out I'd tricked them.

How far could I go in a couple of minutes?

Not far. After only one minute, I had a really bad stitch. I had to stop and take a break.

That was when I heard it. The snowmobile had started up again. But it sounded like it was ahead of me, not behind.

Was I going in circles?

Suddenly I saw a flash of movement between two trees about fifty metres away. Mystery solved. I'd forgotten there were two snowmobiles. Two snowmobiles and four kidnappers. This was the second pair of kidnappers – the ones from the cable car. They must have changed into white ski suits like the others and were following the tracks of the first snowmobile.

Uh oh!

I was standing in the middle of the tracks.

4

AVALANCHE

They were going way too fast, weaving through the trees at breakneck speed. The driver was watching the tracks in the snow, not what was ahead.

He didn't see me and Tommy until the last moment.

He hauled on the handlebars to avoid running us down. I tried going the other way, but it was impossible to move quickly in the knee-deep snow. All I could do was wrap both arms protectively around the baby prince and turn my back on the approaching snowmobile, hoping my body would shield him from the impact.

WHOMP!

That's what it sounds like when a snowmobile hits

a tree. Somehow the driver had managed to swerve past without hitting me. But he lost control of his big, heavy machine and it flipped, throwing him and his passenger clear. Which was lucky for them. They landed in the soft snow next to me. The snowmobile cartwheeled down the steep, slippery slope and slammed into a tree.

For about three seconds there was silence, then . . .

BOOM!

That's what it sounds like when a snowmobile explodes.

It looked amazing. There was a giant ball of yellow flame. Bits of snowmobile and branches went flying into the sky, trailing long lines of smoke and sparks behind them. I felt the shock wave from thirty metres away.

Then I felt something else. The ground shook.

And I heard something else – a deep, low rumble, like thunder.

All around me, trees began trembling. A sudden shower of snow fell from their leaves and branches.

The kidnapper nearest me sat up. He frowned at the other kidnapper, who was rubbing his shoulder.

'What's going on?' he asked.

'Earthquake?' suggested the other man.

But it wasn't an earthquake, it was something worse. Something I'd seen before, on a skiing trip to the South Island of New Zealand.

'It's an avalanche,' I said, rising to my feet. 'Quick, climb up the hill.'

Both the kidnappers looked at me with startled expressions, as if they'd forgotten I was there. I shouldn't have attracted attention to myself. The man nearest me leapt up and grabbed my arm.

'Why go *up*?' he asked. 'If it's an avalanche, won't it come *down* the mountain?'

'The explosion set it off.' I pointed in the direction of the wrecked snowmobile. 'It'll probably start down there.'

There was another rumble, louder than the first one. This time I didn't just feel the ground move, I *saw* it move. Just downhill from where we stood, a long blue line appeared in the snow. It slowly grew wider, until there was a deep trench running right across the slope.

Then, with a rumble that made my teeth rattle, everything below the trench – a patch of snowy hillside roughly the size of a city block – began sliding into the steep valley below us.

'Crikey!' muttered the man holding my arm.

'I've never seen anything like it!' gasped the other one.

For a few seconds they forgot all about me. It was the distraction I needed. Steadying Tommy with my free arm, I flung myself sideways, away from my captor. He wasn't ready for it. His gloved hand lost its grip on my shoulder and I was free.

'Hey!' he yelled, stumbling clumsily after me.

I tried to get past him, heading uphill, but the other kidnapper anticipated my move and cut off my escape route.

I whirled around and went flat out in the other direction. Back down the slope. The kidnappers were right behind me, puffing and cursing as they blundered through the heavy snow. I couldn't let them catch me. Couldn't let them get Tommy.

With a giant leap, I flew across the widening trench and landed safely on the other side.

But how safe was that?

I'd jumped *into* the avalanche.

5
GAME OVER

It was just like being on a moving island. Everything around me was sliding down the mountainside. Not just the snow, but the trees as well. They toppled like matchsticks, mowed down by the avalanche. It was a million-tonne tsunami of snow and ice. Nothing could stand in its way.

And it was moving faster every second. So was I.

I looked back at the kidnappers, two tiny figures standing on a bank of solid snow where the avalanche had started. What had I been thinking? Tommy would have been safer if I'd left him with them. No amount of ransom money would bring a dead prince back to life.

But he wasn't dead yet, and neither was I.

We would be soon if I didn't do something. We were sinking. I was buried to my hips in a rushing, tumbling, heaving sea of snow and ice. It was like being caught in an ocean rip. All I could do was hug Tommy to my chest and try to stay upright. I had to keep our heads clear. If the avalanche dragged us under, we'd be history. Tommy peered out through the narrow gap of my ski-suit zipper like a frightened joey. It looked like he was crying but I couldn't hear him. There was too much other noise. The hiss of sliding snow. The *boom boom boom* of tree trunks snapping. The rumble of a whole mountainside on the move.

Suddenly there was an extra loud *BOOM,* and a huge grey shape splashed into the snow next to me. It was a mountain ash. They're the biggest trees in the forest. Its broken trunk towered over me like the hull of a ship, rocking and swaying as it was swept along by the awesome power of the avalanche.

Then it happened. I started going under. A whirlpool of icy snow wrapped around me, spinning me, tugging me down. It was too big to fight. Too powerful. I felt like

24

an ant caught in rapids. Totally helpless. I couldn't see anything. Could barely breathe. When I tried to gulp in air, my lungs filled with ice.

And what about Tommy? I thought. Could he breathe? Was my jacket keeping the ice out of his mouth?

I screamed. Or tried to. Something crunched into my back, turning my scream into a shout of anger. I didn't want to die! Didn't want Tommy to die, either. I felt mad at the avalanche. I wanted to lash out at it. Defend myself. *Fight* it. But you can't fight snow. It just slips through your fingers. So I took my anger out on the thing behind me – the thing pressing against my back. It felt solid. Summing up all the force I could muster, I drove my elbow into it.

Thump!

Luckily the sleeves of my ski suit were padded. And luckily I was wearing two layers of clothing underneath. But it still hurt. Ooow! The pain brought me back to my senses. I realised what was behind me. The trunk of the fallen mountain ash. And I realised something else, too. A tree trunk is solid. It doesn't slip through your fingers like snow. You can grab it.

Fumbling blindly, I found the stump of a broken branch. I grabbed hold and pulled myself up through the press of smothering snow. There was another branch higher up. And another one just above that. Feeling my way from branch to branch, and being very careful not to crush Tommy between me and the tree, I climbed out of the avalanche onto the wide, rocking trunk of the mountain ash.

It was totally wild! The huge fallen tree was careering down the mountainside, riding the avalanche like a surfboard. With me and Tommy on top, safe from the churning white chaos all around us. But it didn't feel safe. The tree bucked and swayed and jolted. At any moment, I expected it to go nose-down into a sudden gully, or roll over, or ram into something and spill us into the swirling snow. But our giant surfboard held its course. It flew over every gully and smashed through every obstacle, all the way to the bottom of the valley.

Finally the avalanche emptied onto a flat river plain and spread across it like a spilled, million-litre vanilla slushy. A *dirty* vanilla slushy – the churned snow was littered with torn-up boulders, branches, logs, whole trees.

The trunk of our mountain ash came to rest overhanging the river.

In the sudden stillness that followed, the loudest sound was a wailing baby.

'We made it, Tommy,' I gasped, and gave him a finger-tip to suck on.

I was shaking from cold – or maybe with delayed shock after our narrow escape – and my teeth were rattling. And there was a burbling river ten metres below us. So even when Tommy stopped crying, I didn't notice the other noise straightaway.

But after a few seconds it was unmistakable – a tiny drone, like a wasp, getting louder. Uh oh.

It was a two-stroke engine.

I looked back up the mountain. The snowmobile was about four hundred metres away, weaving down through the trees beside the wide, ploughed-up scar left by the avalanche. Sunlight flashed on the passenger's ski goggles as she turned her head in our direction. She tapped the driver on the shoulder and pointed.

They'd seen us.

'We're out of here!' I said to Tommy.

But where else could we go?

Across the river. The snowmobile wouldn't be able to follow us. But how would I get across? The water looked really cold. I could see a crust of ice along the opposite bank. If my socks got wet – and they certainly would – I'd risk losing my toes to frostbite. And the risk to Tommy was even worse. Babies need to stay warm. One slip or wrong step while I crossed the river, and Tommy would get a dunking in the freezing water. He'd be dead within half an hour.

I couldn't risk Tommy's life again. Already I'd risked it by jumping into the avalanche. That time had been an accident – I was trying to get away from the kidnappers and hadn't thought of the consequences. This time I *had* thought of them. If things went wrong, Tommy would die. And it would be my fault.

So crossing the river wasn't an option.

What else could I do? The snowmobile was getting closer. It was only three hundred metres away. I could never outrun it.

Game over, I thought.

Then I had an idea. The kidnappers were after Tommy,

not me. If I left him next to the giant tree trunk for the kidnappers to find, they wouldn't bother coming after me. I could cross the river and escape. Frozen toes would be better than what the kidnappers might do if they caught me.

Tommy looked up at me with his big blue eyes and blew bubbles around my finger.

I sighed. I couldn't leave him.

'We're in this together, Tommy,' I said.

Pulling my zipper up so the baby prince was warm and snug against my chest, I climbed down off the tree trunk and turned towards the river.

6

GUYS WITH GUNS

I hadn't seen them earlier because the tree trunk partially obscured my view. But when I came slithering down the slope, I noticed a row of small red reflectors poking out of the snow. They were the tops of buried marker posts.

There was a road next to the river. A good two-hundred-metre section of it was buried under the avalanche. Further along, a strip of frosty bitumen emerged from the snow and curved around the side of a hill. I quickened my pace. I had no plan other than to reach the unburied section of road before the kidnappers caught up with me.

Maybe snowmobiles can't travel on sealed roads, I thought.

I didn't find out, because I was only halfway there when a blue-and-white campervan came racing around the side of the hill. It had chains on its tyres. They clattered noisily on the bitumen. But not noisily enough to drown out the rising, wasp-like whine of the snowmobile behind me.

'Help!' I cried, waving one arm in the air and supporting Tommy with the other. *'It's an emergency!'*

The van came shuddering to a standstill next to me. A man wearing a yellow-and-brown beanie leaned across from the driver's seat and pushed open the passenger door.

'Jump in,' he said.

I climbed in and slammed the door. 'Do a U-turn,' I cried, gasping for breath. 'We've got to get out of here!'

Beanie Man eyed me strangely. It was hardly surprising. I'd jumped into his campervan and started giving orders.

'There are some guys after me,' I explained. 'Guys with guns.'

The snowmobile was less than a hundred and fifty metres away and closing in fast.

'Hurry!' I said.

Beanie Man seemed unconcerned by my panic. 'How's His Majesty?' he asked.

We both looked down at the bump in my ski suit.

'H-he's okay,' I stammered, confused. How did he know about Prince Thomas?

'Show me,' said Beanie Man.

I opened my collar so he could see Tommy's head.

Beanie Man smiled. But it wasn't the goofy smile of someone looking at a baby. It was an evil smile. Reaching into his jacket, he pulled out a big, snub-nosed pistol and pointed it at me.

'Look, another guy with a gun,' Beanie Man said.

7

END OF THE ROAD

There were five kidnappers, not four. The fifth one – Beanie Man – must have broken into the cable car control room down at the ski lodge. The others would have been in touch with him by mobile phone and told him to stop the cable car when it reached the pylon.

When I escaped with the baby they must have got in touch with him again, and he'd come looking for me. No wonder he looked so pleased with himself. I'd delivered Crown Prince Thomas right into his hands.

But not literally. Not yet. Tommy was still in *my* hands. Dazzled by the sunlight reflecting off the campervan's windscreen, the baby prince started crying again.

I shifted closer to the door to get him out of the glare.

'Don't try anything smart,' warned Beanie Man, waving the big ugly pistol in my face. 'This is a .357 magnum. Have you ever heard one go off?'

I shook my head.

'They make a very loud bang,' he said. 'If I have to shoot you, the noise might damage His Majesty's eardrums. And we don't want that to happen, do we?'

'It's okay,' I said, giving Tommy a fingertip to suck on. 'I'm not going anywhere.'

'Wise choice,' said Beanie Man. 'You never know, if you behave yourself, the boss might take pity on you.'

Then he chuckled. 'But probably not. When I talked to her on the phone, she sounded pretty annoyed at you for running off with His Majesty. In fact, she sounded thoroughly ticked off. And the boss is not a very forgiving lady.'

I was surprised to hear that the kidnappers' boss was female. Probably the woman on the snowmobile. I watched it come racing towards us.

It stopped next to the campervan and the two riders climbed off. The boss ripped off her goggles and helmet and came marching around to my door. She yanked it open.

'Get out!' she snapped.

I climbed gingerly out onto the snow-covered bitumen.

'Give me the baby,' said the boss.

I did as I was told. My hands were shaking. This was the end of the road – not the one I was standing on, but the one I'd been travelling for the past fourteen years. My life. The chilling look in the boss's eyes told me it was almost over.

Tommy started crying again. The boss was holding him awkwardly, like someone who'd never held a baby before.

'You need to support his head,' I told her.

Her face twitched with anger. 'Did I ask for your advice?'

'No. But babies' necks aren't very strong.'

The boss shifted Tommy around so his head rested against her shoulder. It didn't stop him crying.

'Do you have any other suggestions, Mr Mum?' she asked sarcastically.

I shrugged. 'He might be hungry.'

'Shhhh!' said the short man who had been driving

the snowmobile. He was frowning up at the sky with his head tilted to one side, as if he was listening to something. Or trying to listen. Tommy was cranking up the volume.

'*Waah waah waah WAAAAAAAH!*'

With a look of frustration, the boss shoved the crying baby back into my arms. 'See if you can shut him up.'

I gave him my fingertip to suck on, and Tommy stopped crying. Easy as.

But now I could hear something else: *Thwop, thwop, thwop, thwop!*

'Helicopter,' said the short man.

'Do you think it's the police?' asked Beanie Man.

'Whoever it is,' said the boss, 'we don't want them to see us.'

She turned to the small man. 'Peewee, get rid of the snowmobile.'

'Steve,' she said to Beanie Man, 'find somewhere to hide the van while we wait for the others.'

'And you, Mr Mum,' she said, grabbing my arm, 'come with me.'

The boss led me around the side of the campervan and tugged open the door. 'Get in,' she ordered.

There wasn't much room. The narrow, caravan-like interior was crammed with gear – crates, boxes, folding chairs, sleeping bags. There was even stuff piled on the stove top. I squeezed in next to some cartons on the end of the bed.

'Take care of the baby,' the boss said, before slamming the door and locking it.

Tommy and I were plunged into semi-darkness. A pile of cartons was stacked against one of the windows, and a flowery curtain was drawn across the other one. It was nice to be out of the glare of the snowy landscape. Nice to still be alive.

Mr Mum, I thought. As long as I took care of Tommy, the kidnappers probably wouldn't hurt me. But I'd never actually looked after a baby before, only watched Aunty Erin.

A shiver ran through me.

'Please don't poo your nappy, Tommy,' I said nervously.

The campervan rocked as the boss climbed in next to Beanie Man, who I now knew as Steve. She said something to him and the engine roared into life. I held onto Tommy and braced my back against the cartons as the

campervan made a wobbly three-point turn, then accel-
erated down the road with a loud clatter of tyre chains.

Tommy started crying again. I offered him a series of
fingertips to suck on, but he didn't want any of them.
I didn't blame him. The past half-hour had been pretty
traumatic. Falling out of a cable car; taking a massive
wipe-out in the snow at over a hundred kilometres per
hour; riding on an avalanche – it was lucky he was just a
baby and didn't understand what was going on.

But I did. And I had a bad feeling that the *next* half-
hour was going to be even worse.

8
ROADBLOCK

The campervan slowed and stopped. We'd been driving for less than five minutes. Its engine kept running. I heard a helicopter flying low overhead. *Thwop, thwop, thwop, thwop.* Then all I heard was Tommy.

'*Waah waah waaaaaah!*'

I knew the boss and Steve would be able to hear him, too.

'Chill out, little dude,' I whispered, 'or the boss might get someone else to look after you.'

And that would be the end of Mr Mum.

How do you stop a baby crying? I thought desperately.

Feed him, said the little voice in my head.

39

What with?

Change his nappy, then.

No way! I'd never changed a nappy in my life. And you can't change a nappy if you haven't got a clean one to put back on.

Okay, try rocking him.

That was something I could do. I lifted Tommy in my arms and started rocking him like Aunty Erin used to do with Nissa.

No joy. Tommy kept crying.

Sing to him.

I'm not a very good singer, but it was worth a try. Softly, so the kidnappers in the front wouldn't hear, I started singing. Amazingly, Tommy seemed to like it. After three verses of *Mary had a little lamb*, he stopped crying.

I didn't know many baby songs, so I started changing the words. *Mary had a little prince, Rockabye Tommy, The wheels of the campervan go round and round.* For a while, it took my mind off what was going on.

But the wheels of the van *weren't* going round and round. It sat there with its engine running. I didn't hear the helicopter again. At one stage there were clinking sounds outside, like someone fiddling with the tyre chains. I kept rocking Tommy and singing to him. It was cold in the back of the campervan. I grabbed one of the sleeping bags and wrapped it around us.

Finally, I heard voices. A key turned in the lock and the door swung open. It was no longer so glary outside. The campervan was parked under a tree – I guess to hide it from the helicopter. There was bush all around us, and grey clouds had moved across the sun. Three men climbed in the back with me and Tommy – the two men from the cable car, who I'd last seen at the top of the avalanche, and the small man called Peewee. All three were puffing noisily, as if they'd been running. Their breath fogged the chilled air. It was a squeeze to fit everyone in. The two men from the cable car settled themselves in the narrow floor space, Peewee squashed in next to me.

I'd stopped singing as soon as the door opened, and that set Tommy off again.

'*Waah waah waah waah!*'

'What's *wrong* with that baby?' asked the boss, looking in. She'd removed her white ski suit and was wearing

41

a pink quilted jacket, a matching pink hat with fluffy ear-warmers, and jeans. She no longer looked like a kidnapper; she looked like a normal woman out for a day in the snow.

'I think he's hungry,' I said.

'Well, feed him, Mr Mum.'

'What with?'

The boss waved a hand at all the gear piled around us. 'You'll find everything you need in here somewhere.'

Then she slammed the door, plunging us into semi-darkness. I heard the front door close, and the campervan lurched into motion.

I'd hoped the movement might soothe Tommy, but it made his crying worse.

'*WAAH WAAH WAAH WAAAAAAH!*'

Peewee jabbed me with his elbow. 'You heard the boss – feed the little bludger.'

'What with?' I asked again.

One of the other men pointed. 'There's milk in that esky near your foot,' he said.

A plastic cooler was jammed between two cartons. Inside were twelve baby bottles filled with white liquid.

I asked Peewee to hold Tommy while I opened one of the bottles and tried to fit the teat. It was a bit tricky in the bumping, swaying vehicle and I spilt some on Peewee's leg.

'Be careful, you clumsy idiot!'

'Sorry,' I said, but I didn't mean it.

Peewee screwed up his nose and quickly handed Tommy back. 'He stinks!'

Uh oh, I thought.

'There are nappies in that box behind you,' said the man who'd pointed out the esky.

I looked behind me. There was an entire carton of disposable nappies. Now I had no excuse not to change Tommy. But I didn't want to do it.

'I'll feed him first,' I said.

Tommy kept turning his head away. He didn't want to drink. Probably because the milk was stone cold. Then it occurred to me that the baby prince might never have drunk from a bottle before. But he needed a feed. I kept pushing the rubber teat into his mouth. Finally he got the idea and started sucking.

'Thank heavens for that!' sighed Peewee.

'Good onya, Mr Mum,' said the third kidnapper – the one who'd been silent until that moment.

I felt proud of myself. And relieved. They might be kidnappers, but underneath they were just ordinary men.

Maybe they wouldn't kill me when this was over.

That's if Steve didn't kill us all first. He was driving like a maniac. The big, top-heavy campervan was hammering along the road at breakneck speed. It swayed around corners like a rally car, tyres squealing. I could no longer hear the clank and rattle of tyre chains. Steve and the boss must have removed them while the van was hidden under the trees. That meant we were heading out of the snow country.

Where are we going? I wondered.

Suddenly the campervan slowed down. There were two loud thumps on the partition between the driver's cabin and the van's rear section. It sounded like a warning. The three kidnappers in with me exchanged scared looks. One of them stood up and made a tiny gap in the curtains.

'Police!' he hissed.

Peewee pressed something against my ribs. I didn't have to look down to know what it was. 'Not a peep out of you,' he warned, as the van came to a standstill.

There were voices outside, and the crackle of a radio.

I smiled, despite the pistol. The boss and her gang must have spent weeks planning their daring kidnap, but they hadn't put enough thought into how they'd get away afterwards. News of their crime must have spread across the airwaves within minutes of it happening, and the police had sprung into action.

We were at a roadblock.

9

HOOLEY DOOLEY!

I heard the crunch of boots on gravel, then a man's voice outside the driver's door.

'Good afternoon, sir.'

'G'day, officers,' said Steve. He sounded friendly and relaxed, which really surprised me. 'What's happening?'

'There's been an incident back up the mountain and we're checking all vehicles leaving the area.'

Yay! I thought.

Around me, the three kidnappers seemed to hold their breath.

'What kind of incident?' the boss asked, in a sweet, girly voice I hadn't heard before.

'A kidnapping, madam. Princess Monica's baby has been abducted.'

'Oh, how awful!' gasped the boss. 'Who would do such a terrible thing?'

'That's what we're trying to find out, madam,' said a second policeman. 'Would you mind telling us what you're doing in the area?'

Look in the back, I thought, trying to project my thoughts through the thin walls of the campervan to the two policemen outside.

'It's our honeymoon,' Steve said. 'We got married last Saturday.'

'Congratulations,' said both policemen.

I listened in disbelief. The police had fallen for it! They were searching for a gang of kidnappers wearing ski suits, not a just-married couple driving a campervan.

'I can't believe they've taken that sweet little baby,' the boss said. She sounded like she was almost crying. What an actor!

'Don't worry, madam,' said the first policeman, 'we're doing everything in our power to find him.'

Look in the back!

'What kind of lowlife scum would kidnap a baby?' Steve muttered.

Your kind, I thought. Only the pistol pressed against my ribcage kept me silent.

'We're doing our best to catch them,' said the first policeman.

'Enjoy the rest of your honeymoon,' said the second policeman.

I couldn't believe it. They were letting us go!

Tommy must have sensed the tension in my body, because suddenly he jerked away from the bottle and let out a squawk. With the speed of a striking cobra, Peewee brought his other hand up and clamped it across Tommy's face.

'Don't!' I whispered, trying to wrench the hand away. 'You'll suffocate him!'

Peewee jabbed the pistol so hard into my ribs that I nearly cried out in pain.

'Shut *up*!' he hissed in my ear. 'If the police open that door, you're dead.'

Time seemed to stand still. All I could hear was the roar of my pulse in my ears. All I could think about was

Tommy not being able to breathe. The three kidnappers were frozen like statues. Had the policemen heard us? If they had – and if they came to investigate – the next sound might be the last thing I ever heard. The muzzle blast of a .357 magnum.

After what seemed like forever but was probably only a couple of seconds, there was a clunk of gears and the rumble of the campervan's engine. Next moment, we moved slowly through the roadblock.

'Phew!' breathed one of the kidnappers in the back with me.

We heard the boss and Steve laughing in the front. But I wasn't laughing.

'Get your hand off the baby,' I said to Peewee.

'Says who?' he asked, giving me another vicious prod with the pistol.

'He can't breathe!'

'Peewee, lay off!' said one of the others. 'The last thing we want is a dead prince.'

Peewee gave a cruel laugh. But he took his hand away. Tommy's tiny face was white. For a horrible moment, I thought he was dead. Then he coughed and spluttered a couple of times, his face went from white to pink, and he started screaming.

I lifted him to my shoulder and rocked gently from side to side, patting his back like Aunty Erin used to do when Nissa was upset. Tommy howled.

'He sounds perfectly healthy to me,' sneered Peewee, sliding his pistol back inside his ski suit.

I bit the inside of my lip to stop myself from telling Peewee what I thought of him. It wasn't nice. Instead, I talked softly to Tommy.

'There, there, little guy. It's going to be okay. Nobody's going to hurt you.'

Tommy hiccupped, then burped.

'He's pretty bad-mannered for a prince,' joked Peewee.

I ignored him and concentrated on Tommy. He'd stopped crying. It must have been wind that was upsetting him, not what Peewee had done. I tried him with the bottle again, but this time the baby absolutely refused to drink.

'Get me a nappy,' I said to Peewee.

'Get it yourself, Mr Mum.'

I shrugged. 'Okay. You hold the baby, and I'll get it.'

I was bluffing. No way was I going to let Peewee get his hands on Tommy again after what had just happened, but the kidnapper didn't know that. He ripped open the carton and handed me a nappy.

'Thanks,' I said. 'Now give me a bit of room.'

This time Peewee didn't argue. He slid quickly off the bed and joined the others on the floor. I set Tommy on his back and began undoing his clothing. There was lots of it, layer after layer. Princess Monica had him rugged up like an Eskimo. Finally, I reached the nappy.

Hooley dooley! What a pong!

Holding my breath, I peeled back the final layer.

10
WHO'S THE WUSS?

The three kidnappers turned their heads the other way for the entire time I changed Tommy. I was glad they weren't watching – because I didn't do a very good job. It was messy. And I wrecked two nappies before I worked out how to do up the little sticky tags on the sides.

'Nice work, Mr Mum,' one of the kidnappers said when finally I got the job done. It was the man who'd told Pee-wee off for nearly smothering the baby prince. He seemed nicer than the others.

'Thanks,' I said. And gave him a smile – not because I liked him (I didn't), but because I wanted him to like me.

If he liked me, I thought, he might stand up for me at

crunch time – when the boss decided I was no longer any use to them.

The campervan slowed and made a sharp right-hand turn. I felt the wheels leave the smooth bitumen and crunch onto gravel. One of the kidnappers stood up and peeped through the curtains.

'Sawpit Road,' he said.

It was an unusual name. I added it to the list of names already in my head – Peewee, Steve, a woman called 'the boss'. It wasn't a long list, but everything I learned about the kidnappers and where they were taking me and Tommy might be useful later on.

We rattled along Sawpit Road for three or four minutes. Then we slowed again and turned left off the gravel road onto what felt like a bumpy dirt track. Steve drove at a crawling pace. The campervan swayed and creaked like a ship in a storm. Leaves brushed against the sides, branches scraped along the roof. We must have been in a forest, following an overgrown fire trail or four-wheel-drive track. I wedged myself between two boxes and tried to cushion Tommy from the worst of the bumps and jolts. Just his head poked out of my ski suit.

His eyes were closed. He was fast asleep.

Poor little kid, I thought. He'd had a rough day.

The nice kidnapper winked at me. 'Nearly there,' he said.

I wasn't sure if that was good news or not. Because 'there' could only be one place – the kidnappers' hide-out.

What would they do with me when we got there?

We crossed a ricketty wooden bridge. The planks rattled under our wheels. I heard a river below us.

Then I heard another sound – the rasping whine of a chainsaw.

Steve slammed on the brakes so suddenly that Tommy's empty bottle rolled off the bed and clattered to the floor. The three kidnappers in the back with us looked at each other in alarm.

'Hear that?' asked Peewee.

'Sounds like a chainsaw,' said one of the others.

Steve switched off the engine and we heard him talking to the boss.

'. . . must be someone collecting firewood,' he said.

'Shhhh!' said the boss.

We all held our breath and listened, but the chainsaw had fallen silent. The only sounds were the burbling river and the distant laughter of a kookaburra.

'Get the truck out of sight,' the boss said. 'We can't afford to be seen.'

Steve started the engine and the campervan lurched forward. But we hadn't travelled very far when we stopped again. I heard the passenger door creak open, then bang closed as the boss got out. There was a squealing noise, like rusty hinges, from in front of the vehicle. Steve edged it forward a few more metres, then killed the engine. The rusty hinges squealed again – from behind us this time – and everything went dim.

The door at the rear of the campervan swung open. The boss peered in. 'Everybody out,' she said softly.

I climbed stiffly out behind the others. The van was parked inside a big, echoey building, surrounded by rusty machinery. Rising from one of the machines was a huge, round saw blade as big as a beach umbrella. We were in an abandoned sawmill.

'Home, sweet home!' said one of the men, having a yawn and a stretch.

'Keep your voice down,' warned the boss. 'We might have company.'

'You mean the guy with the chainsaw?' Peewee waved his pistol. 'I'll take care of him.'

'Don't be an idiot.'

'But he might have seen us.'

'Unlikely,' said the boss. 'The chainsaw didn't sound close.'

'Then why are we whispering?' asked Peewee.

The boss narrowed her eyes at him. 'There are two ways this can go, Peewee. Either we come out of it filthy rich, or we wind up behind bars for a very long time.'

Peewee shrugged. 'I know that.'

'So be a team player. If I say keep your voice down, keep your voice down.'

'Yes, boss.'

She turned to me. 'How's the baby doing?'

'He's good,' I said. 'I gave him a bottle and now he's sleeping.'

The nice kidnapper patted me on the back. 'He's a man of many talents, this one. He knows how to change nappies and everything.'

'Quite the little mother, aren't you?' said the boss.

I felt my face turn red. 'I was wondering if there's

some way to warm up his next bottle? I'm worried how cold . . .'

That's as far as I got. Because suddenly nobody was paying any attention to me. All five kidnappers were listening to something else. The chainsaw had started up again.

It only ran for a few seconds, then fell silent. But this time it had sounded close.

'Steve, Angelo, Cain – come with me,' the boss said. 'Peewee, stay here and keep an eye on Mr Mum.'

The four of them slipped out through a narrow gap between the sawmill's big double doors. That left me and Tommy alone with Peewee – the least friendly of all five kidnappers. And he didn't look happy about being left behind.

He took his frustration out on me.

'Quite the little mother, aren't you?' he said, mimicking the boss's voice.

I didn't say anything. It didn't seem worth it, seeing as I was looking down the barrel of his pistol.

'Cat got your tongue, wussy boy?' he taunted.

I guess he had a reason to dislike me – I'd kicked

snow in his face up on the mountain, sending him head-first into a clump of saplings. But nobody had ever called me a wuss before.

'If you didn't have a pistol,' I said, 'and I didn't have a baby, we'd find out who's the wuss.'

Something seemed to spark at the back of Peewee's eyes. A tiny grin drew his lips back, exposing small, narrow teeth. He reminded me of a rat.

'Want to try me, do you?' he asked.

Peewee and I were evenly matched in body size, but he was an adult. Fourteen-year-olds don't have the muscles of men. But I did have an orange belt in karate. This could be my chance to escape from the kidnappers. The other four were outside. It was just me and Peewee.

'Only if you get rid of the pistol,' I said.

I didn't think he would do it. But Peewee turned, walked across to the hulk of the giant saw and laid his pistol on its rusty engine casing. Then he came back, pumping his fists like a boxer.

I hoped he wasn't really a boxer.

'No pistol,' Peewee said, showing me his empty hands. 'Your move, Mr Mum.'

There was no way out of it. I had to fight him. Heart racing, I stepped up into the campervan and made a nest out of sleeping bags on the floor where the kidnappers had been sitting. My hands were shaking. Removing Tommy from the front of my ski suit, I settled him snugly among the sleeping bags. He made a soft gurgling sound, but didn't wake up.

'Wish me luck,' I whispered, and touched one of his rosy pink cheeks with my fingertip.

Then I went out to face Peewee.

11

ANGER MANAGEMENT

Peewee raised his fists. They were large compared to the rest of him. And knobbly. He *did* look like a boxer.

A shiver ran through me.

'Hang on,' I said.

I sat down on the metal step below the campervan's doorway and began unclipping my ski boots.

'Getting cold feet?' Peewee jeered.

I let him have his joke. Cold feet were better than clumsy feet. It was hard enough just *walking* in ski boots. Fighting in them would be impossible. I removed my socks as well – all three pairs. Karate is a barefoot sport. Your feet are weapons.

I had another weapon, too. Psychology. My karate instructor had taught me to fight with my brain as well as my body. *Study your opponent and find his weaknesses*, he'd advised. *Then use his weaknesses against him.*

Peewee had anger management problems. I'd known him for only a couple of hours, but already I'd seen him lose his temper – or come close to losing it – on four occasions.

It was time for number five.

'Why do they call you Peewee?' I asked. 'Is it because you've got a really small brain?'

Something in Peewee seemed to snap. His eyes bugged out, his jaw quivered, his face turned red. He muttered something under his breath – it sounded more like an animal snarl than a word – then charged.

If Peewee had any boxing skills to begin with, they totally disappeared when he lost his temper. Instead of attacking with his fists, he rushed at me with fingers splayed, as if he wanted to claw my eyes out. Or wrap his big hands around my neck and throttle me. I didn't wait to find out. Twisting around, I put up an elbow block and hit him in the kidney area with a spinning side kick.

61

He grunted and doubled over, slumping against the campervan to stop himself falling.

'Had enough?' I asked.

Peewee didn't answer. His shoulders heaved and his breath came in big, whistling sobs.

'You'd better sit down,' I said, scared I'd hit him too hard.

I needn't have worried. Suddenly, Peewee pushed himself away from the campervan and hurled himself at me like a pro wrestler bouncing off the ropes.

There wasn't time to think, only to react. I met Peewee's attack with a double front snap kick to his midsection, and followed up with a forearm strike to his chin. Peewee went down like a sack of cement.

He was out for the count.

I was pumped. I'd taken on a man in unarmed combat and beaten him fair and square!

But I'd only won the battle, I hadn't won the war (as my father would say). There were four more kidnappers outside, all of them armed. I ran to the giant saw and picked up Peewee's pistol. That evened things up a bit. But it was still four against one – impossible odds. If it came to a shoot-out, I'd have no chance.

I had to get away before the others came back.

But I couldn't leave Tommy behind.

I ran back to the campervan and yanked the driver's door open. Thank you, Steve! He'd left the key in the ignition. Putting the pistol carefully on the passenger seat, I climbed in and started the engine. I'd forgotten to open the big sawmill doors but that didn't matter. They weren't locked. I could smash my way out. I clunked the transmission into reverse and gave it some juice.

Then I remembered something else I'd forgotten – Peewee. He was lying directly behind the campervan. I'd been about to drive over him!

Applying the handbrake, I jumped out and charged around the back. Peewee was sitting up, massaging his neck and turning his head stiffly from side to side.

'I'm going to reverse the truck,' I said. 'You'd better get out of the way.'

Peewee stopped working on his neck and stretched both hands towards me. 'Can you help me up? I can't move my legs.'

He was bluffing. I could see the cunning look in his

weasly eyes. He just wanted me to go close enough so he could grab me.

'You've got ten seconds,' I said.

I turned to close the campervan's rear door. And nearly tripped on my boots and socks lying on the concrete below the step. I'd forgotten all about them in my panic to get away before the other kidnappers returned. Forgotten I was barefoot. My toes were freezing! But cold toes were the least of my problems. The boss and the others could be back at any moment. I flung my boots and socks in the back with Tommy and slammed the door.

Too late. I heard a scuffling noise behind me and started to turn my head.

The last thing I saw was a huge knobbly fist, coming at me like a sledgehammer.

WHAM!

12

DR MUM

I woke up lying flat on my back in a tiny room. The walls were made of brick, the sloping roof was rusty iron. There was a small grimy window high on one wall. A washbasin was bolted to another wall and my head rested against something smooth and hard and cold. I blinked up at the curve of white china above me and realised where I was – in a toilet.

Locked in a toilet, I soon discovered. The door rattled but wouldn't open.

I had a thumping headache and the entire right side of my face felt swollen and bruised. So much for beating Peewee in unarmed combat. I'd won round one, but he'd

65

come back at the beginning of round two with a knock-out punch. Well, maybe slightly *before* the beginning of round two, but the result couldn't be contested.

I'd been TKO'd.

I felt dizzy and had to sit down on the toilet seat until the spinning sensation stopped. It was cold. My bare toes were halfway to becoming ice cubes and I could see my breath. I blew on my hands to warm them. According to my watch, it was 5.05 in the afternoon. I looked up at the window. The top of a tree and a small patch of grey sky were visible through the discoloured glass. I stood on the toilet seat to see what else was outside. Lots more trees, with ferns growing beneath them, and a shed. The shed looked a lot newer than the sawmill. Made of corrugated iron, it was about the size of a double garage. There was a roller door at one end and, above it, a sign partly obscured by an overhanging branch. I rubbed the glass to clear it, but most of the grime was on the outside. Straining my eyes, I could just make out two words: KING CLUB. Weird.

Suddenly I heard a chainsaw. The noise seemed to come from the King Club. It revved about three times and stopped, replaced by the crazy laughter of a kookaburra. Next I heard a seagull, then a black cockatoo.

A large brown bird came stalking around the corner of the shed. It was the size of a rooster, with a long brown-and-white tail. It stopped near the roller door, spread its tail like a fan, and started shaking it. The chainsaw revved again. It took me a couple of seconds to realise that what I was seeing and what I was hearing went together. The bird was making the chainsaw noise!

It was a lyrebird. They're the world's best mimics. They can imitate almost any sound they hear. This lyrebird must have heard a chainsaw once. And a barking dog, because that's what it did next. Then it warbled like a magpie.

Suddenly the lyrebird lowered its tail. Head tilted, it seemed to peer in my direction. Then it shot back around the side of the shed and disappeared into the ferns.

Two figures came running into view from almost below me. It was Steve and the 'nice' kidnapper – Angelo. They both carried pistols. Steve opened the roller door and looked into the shed. Angelo ran around the back. They were searching for someone with a chainsaw.

Search all you like, I thought, you're not going to find anyone. It made me smile. That was a mistake. Smiling *hurt*. The right half of my face felt like a giant bruise.

Several minutes later, the two kidnappers came walking back towards the sawmill. They'd put their pistols away and both men were smiling.

'It sounded so *real*!' Angelo said.

Steve laughed. 'Wait till the boss finds out we've spent half the day hiding from a smart-mouthed bird!'

Angelo passed within three metres of my window. I thought about tapping on the glass and asking for food – suddenly I was *starving* – but decided not to attract attention to myself. A plan was forming in my mind. As long as the kidnappers thought I was unconscious, they would leave me alone. Once it got dark, I might be able to break the window and escape.

There was a scraping noise on the other side of the door. Before I could drop to the floor and pretend to be unconscious, the door creaked open and Peewee stood there.

So much for my plan.

'The boss wants you,' he said.

Then he followed me with his pistol. I noticed he was limping. He'd think twice before calling me a wuss again.

Peewee didn't have to show me where to go. We were inside the big shadowy sawmill and I could see a light down the other end. I could also hear a radio playing and Tommy crying.

The kidnappers had set up two folding tables next to the campervan. They sat around them on camp chairs while Steve cooked sausages on a portable gas cooker. Soft country music came from a radio on one of the tables, and a hissing lantern dangled from an overhead beam. It looked like a peaceful camping scene, except it was indoors.

But thanks to Tommy, it certainly *wasn't* peaceful.

'Waah waah waah!'

'Look who's back in the land of the living,' the boss said, speaking loudly to make herself heard above Tommy's racket. 'How's your head?'

'Sore,' I said.

The boss aimed a finger at me, like an imaginary gun. 'Play the hero again, and do you know what'll happen?'

I nodded. Next time I played the hero, she and her gang would get what they deserved.

'I'm glad we understand each other,' the boss said. She waved a hand in the direction of the campervan. 'Now make yourself useful, Mr Mum, and shut that baby up.'

I found Tommy on the bed. Someone had made a bassinette for him out of a carton lined with blankets. A mostly full bottle lay next to him, leaking milk into the bedding. But Tommy wasn't interested in milk – and especially not *cold* milk. The poor little guy was so upset his face was nearly purple. One sniff told me what the problem was. The kidnappers were useless! Lifting the baby prince out of the tangled blankets, I carried him out of the van.

'Hey!' Peewee cried, when I plonked Tommy on the table between the bread and a plate of sausages. 'We're trying to eat, here.'

'I've got to change his nappy,' I said, unsnapping a row of buttons.

'Not near the food!' growled the boss.

'I need to see what I'm doing,' I said, peeling off the first layer of Tommy's clothing. 'This is the only bright place.'

It took the kidnappers about five seconds to clear the table. They put everything on the second table, then dragged it several metres from where I was changing Tommy. He'd stopped crying, but he still looked red and angry.

'Someone get me a clean nappy,' I said.

Angelo got up and fetched one from the campervan. He wrinkled his nose.

'Diarrhoea?' he asked, sounding concerned.

It wasn't diarrhoea, it was just a poopy nappy. But the kidnappers seemed to know nothing about babies. I had an idea.

'It's worse,' I said. 'See how red he is? I think he's got a fever.'

Tommy was red because he'd been crying so hard. But Angelo fell for it.

'Hey, boss,' he called. 'The baby's crook.'

The boss came over. She looked down at Tommy with a slightly revolted expression on her face. 'What's the matter with him?'

'He's burning up,' I said, touching his bright red forehead. 'We need to get him to a hospital.'

The boss shook her head. 'He stays here,' she said flatly.

'He might die.'

The boss looked me in the eye. 'How would you like a promotion, Mr Mum?'

I shrugged. What was she talking about?

'From now on you're *Dr* Mum,' the boss said. 'And here's the deal: the baby dies, *you* die.'

13
HERO

Being Dr Mum had its good points. I was no longer locked in the toilet. Now I was locked in the back of the stationary campervan with Tommy. I wasn't worried about him dying, but our captors were. Kidnapping a prince was a really serious crime, but if he died they'd be murderers. That gave me a lot of bargaining power. All I had to do was bang on the door and someone would come to see what I wanted. A freshly warmed bottle for Tommy. Four sausages wrapped in bread (and dripping tomato sauce) for me. A cup of tea. Panadol for my headache. A torch so I could see what I was doing once it got dark. Spare blankets to keep Tommy and me warm. A bucket of warm water, some soap and a towel. They even took away Tommy's used nappies when I asked them to. And Angelo found my socks.

Apart from Tommy waking me every few hours for a feed and a nappy change, I had quite a restful night. But I didn't sleep deeply. Even when my tired body had shut down, part of me remained alert, listening to every noise that filtered through the campervan's thin walls. There was a lot of snoring. The kidnappers had unrolled their sleeping bags on the sawmill floor just outside the van. And the radio stayed on all night. Every half-hour there was a news report, and nearly all the news was about the kidnapping of Crown Prince Thomas.

A massive search was underway. It was the biggest police operation in Australian history, but so far they had no clues.

In later reports there was an interview with Princess Monica, who begged the kidnappers to give her baby back. She even mentioned me, and called me a hero.

The Police Commissioner said I was a hero, too.

It felt strange hearing my name on the radio. The police were also searching for me. They thought I might be dead. I wished I could let everyone know that I was alive, especially Mum and Dad.

At the end of one report, the newsreader said the police were still waiting to hear from the kidnappers. He said Princess Monica and Prince Nicklaus were prepared to pay a million dollars for the safe return of Crown Prince Thomas.

The boss scoffed when she heard this. 'Only *one* million?' she said to the radio. 'Isn't your future king worth more to you than that?'

I was feeding Tommy at the time. Locked in the back of the campervan with the kidnapped crown prince in my arms. And suddenly, for no reason I could think of, I started shaking all over. It was so bad I had to clench my teeth to stop them rattling. Tommy felt me trembling. He pulled away from the bottle and looked up at me. There was a worried expression in his big blue eyes.

'It's okay, little guy,' I whispered, raising him to my shoulder to burp him. 'We'll get out of this somehow.'

A car engine woke me shortly before dawn. It wasn't the campervan; it was outside the sawmill. At first I thought it was the police come to rescue us. But the vehicle wasn't coming, it was going. I heard it rattle across the bridge and drive off into the night.

The kidnappers must have two vehicles, not one. It made sense. They'd need something smaller and less conspicuous than a campervan when they went to collect the ransom money. That was probably where they were going now. Not all of them had gone. I could still hear snoring outside. I wondered who'd gone, and who'd stayed behind.

In the morning, the kidnapper called Cain let me out to have breakfast. It was sausages again, but this time there was toast instead of bread. I noticed that the boss and Steve weren't there.

'How's the baby?' Angelo asked.

'He's fine,' I said, without thinking. I was still half asleep. 'I mean, he hasn't got any worse.'

Angelo sipped his tea. 'You're doing good work, Sam,' he said with a smile.

He must have heard my name on the radio reports. It was nice to be called Sam, not Mr Mum or Dr Mum. It made me like him a bit more.

'I thought I heard a car during the night,' I said casually.

'That was the boss and Steve.'

'Zip your mouth, Angelo,' Peewee warned.

'Why should I? He'll find out soon enough anyway.'

I looked from Peewee to Angelo. 'Find out what?'

'You're off to school this afternoon,' Angelo said.

14
NO CHOICE

The blazer was a bit tight, but everything else fitted me perfectly. Even the brown leather shoes.

Brown leather shoes!

'Tuck your shirt in,' the boss said.

'You wear them hanging out.'

She shook her head. 'Not at Hobart Grammar. You have to look just like everyone else.'

I was glad I didn't go to Hobart Grammar. I felt like a dork in the purple, green and yellow uniform. But the boss was right – I needed to blend in with the crowd. If this went wrong, Princess Monica and Prince Nicklaus would never see their baby son again.

The boss and Steve had returned at lunchtime. Instead of collecting the ransom money, they'd been shopping for clothes. A school uniform for me, football supporters' gear for them. Now Steve had a Hawthorn jacket and scarf to match his yellow-and-brown beanie, and the boss was decked out all in blue and white like a Geelong supporter.

Before sending me into the campervan to get changed, the boss had explained what was going on. I wasn't going to school, I was going to the footy. Two of the AFL's top clubs, Hawthorn and Geelong, were playing in Hobart that afternoon. It was a special promotion for the Government's brand new health program aimed at kids, *Sport in Schools*. Anyone wearing their school uniform would be allowed in free. And so would their parents. The boss, Steve and I were going as a family.

'*Why* are we going to the football?' I asked.

'To get the ransom money,' the boss explained. 'And that's where you come into it. You'll be making the pickup.'

My jaw dropped. '*Me?* That's crazy!'

'Not crazy at all. Whoever makes the drop won't be alone – there'll be undercover agents tailing him, or watching from a helicopter. We have to surprise them.

They'll be expecting an adult to collect the money, not a sweet-faced private schoolboy.'

Sweet-faced? I'd peeked at myself in the campervan's mirror earlier. I had a monster black eye and an ugly yellow-and-blue bruise that ran all the way down the right side of my face. 'Who's going to give a million dollars to a fourteen-year-old kid?' I asked.

'They'll do what I tell them,' the boss said. 'And don't even think about double-crossing us. We'll be watching you, too. Say one word to the drop, and nobody will ever see little Prince Thomas again.'

The look in her eyes showed me she meant it.

'Are we taking him with us?' I asked.

'No. Once we've collected the ransom and made sure it's all there, we'll leave him somewhere where the police can find him,' the boss said. 'In the meantime, he can stay here with his Uncle Peewee.'

Peewee, who'd been listening, gave a nasty laugh.

'Can't Angelo look after him?' I said.

Angelo nodded. 'I'll take care of him, Sam.'

It was nice to have a friend, even if he was one of the kidnappers.

'Okay, I'll do it,' I said to the boss. 'I'll pick up the ransom money.'

'You don't have a choice,' she said.

15

A VERY BAD FEELING

The sign on the shed said CROWFORD KAYAKING CLUB, not KING CLUB. Half of it had been hidden behind the trees when I'd looked out the toilet window. As Steve bent to open the roller door, I noticed a snapped padlock lying in the dirt. The kidnappers must have broken into the shed so they could hide their second car. I was right about it being inconspicuous – it was a small green hatchback, the type of car no one would look at twice. Two racks of kayaks had been shoved against the walls to make room for it.

'Would you like to drive us, Mother?' Steve asked, dangling the keys.

The boss laughed. 'No, you drive, Father,' she said.

She held open one of the back doors for me. 'Get in and lie on the floor. Keep your head down.'

I did as I was told. But it seemed silly to be hiding. There was no one around.

After nearly an hour, the boss finally told me I could sit up. I was stiff from lying on the floor and my right arm had pins and needles. We were driving along a quiet suburban street.

'Welcome to Hobart,' said Steve.

Now I realised why they'd made me keep my head down all the way from their hide-out. Not so nobody would see me, but so *I* wouldn't see. They didn't want me to know where their hide-out was, in case something went wrong – like if I got away, or talked to the drop. But I wasn't going to do either of those things. I was going to cooperate with the kidnappers one hundred percent. The boss was right – I didn't have a choice. Tommy's life was on the line.

Mine was, too. I still didn't know what the kidnappers were going to do with me once this was all over. I'd helped them by looking after Tommy – especially when they thought he was sick – and now I was helping them again. I hoped it was enough to make them let me go when this was all over, and not get rid of me permanently.

We turned down another street and came to a small park. Steve drove round behind the toilets. No one was about.

'Get out and stretch your legs,' the boss told me. 'Use the toilets if you need to.'

When I came out, Steve was tying yellow and brown streamers to the car's aerial. The boss was sitting in the passenger seat putting on blue and white face paint. She looked like a fanatical Geelong supporter. It was a good disguise.

Next, she painted Steve's face in the yellow and brown Hawthorn colours.

Then she turned to me. 'Which team are you going for, Mr Mum? Geelong or Hawthorn?'

I shrugged. 'Hawthorn.'

She made me lean against the car while she painted my face in yellow and brown stripes.

'Lovely!' she said, standing back to admire her artwork. 'Even your mum wouldn't know you.'

The boss threw the face-painting gear into the car and pulled out a large black backpack.

'Put it on,' she said.

The backpack was very light. 'What's in it?' I asked, threading my arms through the straps.

'Nothing,' the boss said, mysteriously. 'But there will be.'

As we drove out of the park, we must have looked like a normal family on their way to the football. I wished we were. My palms were sweaty and I'd started shaking again. Despite all the boss's careful plans, a thousand things could go wrong. Even if they didn't, I had a very bad feeling about how this was going to end. Maybe not for Tommy, he was just a baby. But I'd spent twenty-four hours with the kidnappers. Except for the boss, I knew all their first names. And I knew what they looked like.

They weren't going to let me go.

16

NEEDLE IN A HAYSTACK

Steve pulled over to the kerb. I could see the stadium rising above the rooftops about a kilometre away. I wondered why we'd stopped. It was just after four o'clock in the afternoon. Unless the game had started late, it would be over in half an hour.

The boss tapped a number into her mobile phone. 'Football stadium, ten minutes,' she said in a disguised voice, then snapped the phone shut.

I guessed she was speaking to the drop – probably an undercover agent or a plain-clothes policeman. She and Steve must have arranged it when they came to town that morning. They would have told the drop to have the ransom money ready and be waiting for their next call – the one the boss had just made. By telling them the drop-off point at the very last moment, there wasn't time for the police to get there before us and set up a trap.

We sat in the car for five minutes. Then the boss nodded and Steve drove off. Half a block from the stadium, Steve steered the hatchback into a crowded car park. It was packed – there were no empty spaces. As we cruised slowly between the rows of cars – nearly all of them with coloured streamers on their aerials like ours – the boss twisted around and handed me a mobile phone. It wasn't the one she'd used to talk to the drop.

'Put this in your pocket,' she said. 'We've fixed it so it can't make outgoing calls, but we'll know if you try. Go to the stadium and wait just inside the main gate.'

'Then what do I do?' I asked nervously.

'I'll phone you and let you know,' the boss said. 'Make sure you're there in five minutes.'

She told Steve to stop the car. Wearing the backpack, I opened my door and got out. The boss wound down her window.

'Don't try anything,' she warned. 'We'll be watching your every move.'

Walking away from the kidnappers' car gave me the strangest feeling. I was free, but I wasn't. If I didn't collect the ransom money, Prince Thomas might never be seen again. The hairs on my neck stood up and my palms were sweaty. I was terrified something would go wrong.

Ohmygosh! A policeman and a policewoman stood on the pavement outside the stadium. They were looking right at me, watching me approach. It was too late to stop, too late to look for another entrance. If I changed direction now, it would look like I was guilty of something. And I *was* guilty of something – helping the kidnappers get their money.

As I crossed the wide street towards the two police officers, my heart rate increased to about two hundred beats per minute. I felt sure they'd recognise me. I was a Missing Person – the 'young hero' who'd caught Prince Thomas when he fell out of the cable car and then tried to escape from the kidnappers. My photo would be in all the newspapers and in every police station around the country. I was famous.

But in the photo I wouldn't be dressed as a Hobart Grammar student. My face wouldn't be caked with yellow and brown paint.

Was the disguise going to work?

The policewoman smiled as I walked past. 'You're a bit late, aren't you?' she said with a friendly smile.

I smiled, too, but I didn't say anything. The boss and Steve were watching from the car park. If they saw me talking to the police, they might get the wrong idea.

A huge roar went up from the crowd inside the stadium. Someone must have kicked a goal. Even though the game wasn't over, people were leaving already, probably to get to their cars before the big rush after the final siren. There were quite a few kids in school uniform. It made me feel less conspicuous as I jostled my way through the gates, going in the opposite direction.

I found myself at the mouth of a wide tunnel leading under the stands. A few people were coming out, but most stood at the other end with their backs to me, watching the final moments of the game. I heard another loud cheer, then a boo as something happened on the field that the crowd didn't like.

My mobile rang. 'Where are you?' the boss asked.

'Just inside the gates.'

'The drop's on his way. You should see him come through the gates any moment. He's got a red-and-black beanie on, and he's wearing a backpack.'

Right on cue, a man in a grey tracksuit wearing a red-and-black beanie came pushing through the crowded entrance. He carried a bulky blue backpack slung across his shoulder. A backpack full of money. A tingle ran up and down my spine. It was really happening. They were going to pay the ransom.

And I was the pickup.

The drop's eyes darted left and right, but he didn't give me a second glance. He wasn't expecting the pickup to be a schoolboy.

'I can see him,' I whispered into my mobile.

'Follow him,' the boss said. 'He'll go into the stadium and pretend to watch the game. He'll put the backpack on the ground. Come up behind him and say, "Prince Thomas." Then pick up the backpack.'

'What if he tries to stop me?' I asked, nervously.

'He won't. Walk calmly away and blend into the crowd.

Make sure nobody's following you. Find some toilets and transfer everything from his backpack into yours. Wait there till the game's over, then leave the stadium with the crowd. I'll make contact when you get outside. Have you got all that?'

I wasn't sure. It sounded complicated. 'I guess so,' I said.

'Don't stuff up,' the boss warned. 'We'll be watching you.'

It was easy following the drop, even in the crowd. He must have been the only person in the stadium wearing a red-and-black beanie. I stayed ten or fifteen metres behind him all the way along the tunnel. When he reached the end, he turned left into the stands. He found a couple of empty seats at the end of a row and sat down, putting the backpack on the seat next to him. Then he pulled a small pair of binoculars from his jacket pocket and pretended to watch the game.

I walked slowly down the aisle towards him. Everyone seemed intent on the game, but it felt like they were watching me. I heard a helicopter overhead and wondered if it was the police. One of the Hawthorn players took a mark, and about thirty thousand people cheered. I sat down behind the drop and leaned forward.

'Prince Thomas,' I said, my voice going suddenly squeaky.

The drop didn't give any sign to show he'd heard me. He kept his binoculars fixed on the football players.

Reaching across the back of the seat in front of me, I picked up his backpack. This was the moment of truth. I half-expected the drop to swing around, grab my wrist and ask me what the heck I thought I was doing. But he didn't move. He kept his eyes on the game. The Hawthorn player took his kick and a mighty roar filled the stadium.

By the time everyone had stopped cheering, I was halfway to the men's toilets carrying the drop's bulky blue backpack under my arm. It was surprisingly heavy.

I found an empty cubicle and locked the door. I placed the backpack on the toilet lid and undid the zipper. Hooley dooley! It was full of money. More one-hundred-dollar notes than I could count. They were packed in bundles the size of house bricks and bound with rubber bands. With shaking hands, I transferred the ransom money from the blue backpack to the black one the boss had given me. When I was finished, I stuffed the empty one down behind the toilet bowl and put the black bag on my back.

I felt calm as I stepped out of the cubicle. If there were other agents trying to spot me leaving the stadium, they'd be looking for someone with a blue backpack, not a black one. I'd be just another school kid in a crowd that included nearly every school kid in Hobart and the surrounding towns. It'd be like looking for a needle in a haystack.

They'd never find me.

Even though she was a criminal, I had to admire the boss for her clever planning. She had thought of everything.

Well, not quite everything.

'Hey, you,' a voice said behind me. 'Stop right there!'

17
THE WRONG PERSON TO BULLY

There were two of them. They were standing over by the washbasins. They looked like Year Twelves. Both wore the same uniform as me.

'Where's your boater?' said the one with a prefect badge pinned to his blazer.

'My what?' I asked.

'Your hat, idiot!'

They both wore hats – silly-looking, square-topped, imitation straw hats with bands in the purple, green and yellow Hobart Grammar School colours. The boss hadn't got me a hat.

'I left it at home,' I said with a shrug. 'What's it to you?'

'I'll tell you what it is,' Prefect said in a bossy voice. 'It's a uniform infringement.'

I shifted the backpack straps higher on my shoulders. I didn't know how much money was on my back – one million dollars? two million? – but it was really heavy. 'We're not at school now,' I said.

Prefect sniffed. 'When you're wearing the Hobart Grammar uniform, you're representing the school. It doesn't matter where you are, you have to be correctly dressed.'

'It's just a hat,' I said, walking past him to get to the basins.

'It's part of the uniform,' said Prefect. 'I'm putting you on report. What's your name?'

I said the first name that came into my head. 'Tommy.'

'Tommy who?'

'Smith,' I said, busily washing my hands.

The other boy was looking at me in the mirror, trying to see who I was under the face paint. 'Are you new?' he asked.

'I started this term.'

'Who's your form master?'

Uh oh. Now I was in trouble. I turned off the tap and

started moving towards the paper towel dispensers. They were near the door. But Prefect stepped in front of me, blocking my escape.

'We asked you a question, Smith. Who's your form master?'

I looked him in the eye. 'Just let me past,' I said softly. 'Something really important's going down. Way more important than school uniforms.'

'Cut the bull and tell us who your form master is.'

My mobile rang. Perfect timing. 'Excuse me,' I said, pulling it out of my blazer pocket.

It was the boss. 'Have you got the money?' she asked.

'Just a minute,' I said, and held the phone out to Prefect. 'It's for you.'

He was so surprised, he took it.

'H-hello?' he stammered, holding the mobile phone to his ear.

For a second Prefect was concentrating on the phone, not on me. Big mistake. I slammed into him shoulder first, knocking him out of my way. He fell backwards against the wall, tipping over one of the towel bins. The mobile clattered to the floor and went skidding across the tiles. I tried to scoop it up but Prefect's friend was onto me with the speed of a pit bull. Luckily he couldn't fight like a pit bull – in fact, he didn't know how to fight at all. He was much bigger than me but it wasn't an even contest. A simple leg sweep sent him backside first onto the tiles.

Sorry guys, I thought. You picked the wrong person to bully.

But it wasn't over yet. While I'd been grappling with his friend, Prefect had regained his balance. He picked up the metal rubbish bin and hurled it at me. I spun around, deflecting it with a side snap kick. These sturdy brown school shoes were useful, after all.

'You're in *so* much trouble,' Prefect growled, balling his hands into fists and advancing slowly towards me.

I guessed he wasn't talking about putting me on report this time.

'Don't try it,' I warned, crouching into a cat stance. 'I'm a karate black belt.'

I started backing towards the door.

Prefect probably knew I was exaggerating, but he'd seen me deal with his friend and the flying rubbish bin.

Instead of following me, he went to help his friend up off the floor.

The phone started ringing again but I couldn't go back for it. I slipped out the door. And nearly had a heart attack. About ten more Hobart Grammar boys were standing outside. The one nearest me wore a prefect's badge.

'Where's your boater?' he asked.

This time I didn't answer. I simply turned and walked away. Back into the stands, rather than towards the stadium exit where I should have been heading. When I didn't answer the phone, the boss would start to panic. But first I had to get away from the Hobart Grammar boys. My only chance was to lose myself in the crowd.

'Hey, I asked you a question!' called Prefect Number Two.

Of all the schools in Hobart, why had the boss picked Hobart Grammar? I kept walking. But I'd only gone a few more paces before I heard the clatter of running feet. Lots of them. I glanced over my shoulder. They were all after me, about a dozen big, angry Grammar boys, including the first prefect and his friend. I started running, too.

The game had just finished. Everyone was on their feet, filing into the already crowded aisles. I ran the other way, darting and weaving through a crush of bodies with the Grammar boys hot on my heels. People yelled angrily as I barged my way through. Parents dragged their little kids clear.

'Excuse me!' I cried. 'Excuse me! Excuse me!'

I wished I was going the other way. Wished I was part of the huge crowd shuffling slowly towards the exits. The boss would be waiting for me outside. She'd be wondering why I wasn't answering the phone. Wondering and worrying, and maybe thinking I'd double-crossed her.

I hoped she and Steve wouldn't panic and drive off without me.

What would happen to Tommy?

'Excuse me!' I gasped, squeezing between a woman and a little girl in a blue-and-grey school uniform.

The woman gave me a frosty glare. 'Where are your manners?' she growled.

All I could say was, 'Sorry!'

I knew she would forgive me if she knew what was happening. She was a mother – she'd want Princess Monica to get her baby back.

I glanced over my shoulder. Three Grammar boys were

only a few metres behind. They were running single file, pushing through the gap I'd created in the flow of people going the other way. Gaining on me with every stride.

If they caught me, it would be all over, red rover.

There was a crush of bodies ahead. I couldn't get through. So I swerved out of the aisle and ran flat out between two rows of seats. I could hear the pounding feet of a Grammar boy just behind me. A family was coming the other way. I took a running jump and landed in the next row. Another Grammar boy charged towards me from the other end, using the seats as stepping stones. I ran back the other way, but two more Grammar boys closed in from that end. Another five Grammar boys came filing along the next row up.

I was trapped. They had chased me nearly all the way to the front of the stands. There was one more row of seats, then a wall of people standing along the fence at the edge of the wide green playing field. The game was over, but they'd stayed to watch the two teams leave the oval.

I clambered across the front row of seats and pushed my way through the crush of spectators and autograph-hunters to the fence.

And jumped over.

It was about a metre and a half from the top of the fence to the playing surface. The weight of the backpack overbalanced me and I went face down in the grass. There were boos and jeers from the thousands of people still in the stadium. I was too scared to feel embarrassed. I didn't think the Grammar boys would follow me, but now I had other problems.

Three Geelong players were walking in my direction. They were huge and sweaty, and if looks could kill, I'd be dead. I scrambled to my feet and took off along the boundary. One of them said something and the other two laughed. But they didn't come after me. They were heading towards the players' gate, along with all the other players from both teams. I heard a helicopter overhead and looked for somewhere to escape. There was nowhere to hide. Everyone was watching me. Even the big television cameras were swivelling in my direction. I felt like an ant under a microscope.

There was a shout in the distance. Three security men came sprinting across the ground. I found my second wind and ran faster. The crowd cheered. For a couple of seconds I thought they were cheering for me. Then I saw what they saw.

Franky Budd, Hawthorn's star full-forward, had been signing autographs for a group of primary school kids leaning over the boundary fence about a hundred metres from the players' gate. I didn't see him until it was too late.

I tried to swerve around him, but Franky extended a massive hand and grabbed my backpack.

There was a ripping sound, like a zipper giving way, and a wad of one-hundred-dollar notes landed at our feet.

18
WORST DECISION

'Have you robbed a bank?' Franky asked, stooping to pick up the money.

I glanced over my shoulder. The security men had almost reached us. I only had a few seconds.

'It's the ransom money for Prince Thomas. Let me go or they'll kill him.'

They say you need quick reflexes, not a quick brain, to be a football star – but Franky Budd had both. 'Are you the kid in the newspaper?'

I nodded. 'The kidnappers are hiding out in an abandoned sawmill. Tell the police it's near Sawpit Road.'

That was all I had time to say before the first security

man arrived. He was red-faced and out of breath.

'Nice work, Franky,' he puffed. 'I'll take him from here.'

The towering AFL player blocked his path. 'Let him be. He just wants my autograph.'

Turning his back on the security man, Franky slipped the wad of money back into my backpack.

'Put your foot here,' he said, quickly making a stirrup with his enormous hands. As he hoisted me over the fence, Franky said softly, 'Sawpit Road, right?'

'You've got it.'

Ten seconds later I was part of the crowd – one of about twenty thousand school kids filing slowly out of the stadium. I attached myself to a group of Year Sevens or Eights, whose uniform was similar to Hobart Grammar's except they weren't wearing hats. Listening to their conversation, I learned that Hawthorn had won the match with the very last kick.

And guess who kicked it?

'Hey, how cute was that boy who jumped the fence to get Franky Budd's autograph?' a girl in front of me said as we filed through the shadowy tunnel under the stands.

The girl next to her tittered. 'How could you even

tell, Courtney? His face was covered in paint.'

'Yeah, but he had nice hair,' Courtney replied.

As soon as we were out of the tunnel, I separated from Courtney's group. I didn't want any of them – especially Courtney – getting a good look at me. When you're wearing a backpack stuffed full of one-hundred-dollar notes, you don't want people taking notice of you.

Someone tapped me on the shoulder.

I nearly jumped out of my brand new school shoes. 'B-b-boss!' I gasped.

'There you are, darling,' she said, and leaned so close that for a scary moment I thought she was going to kiss me. 'Don't call me boss, I'm your *mother*, remember.'

People jostled past on both sides. Any one of the adults could have been an undercover police officer. Not that I cared any longer. I'd told Franky Budd what was going on, and he would tell the police.

'Where's Dad?' I asked.

'In the car,' the boss said, linking her arm through mine. 'Come along, darling, or we'll be late home for dinner.'

We shuffled through the gates with the rest of the crowd. As soon as we were outside, the boss steered me to the left. We shuffled slowly along the footpath in a sea of people. There were two Hobart Grammar boys not far ahead. Luckily, they didn't look around. The mass of people gradually thinned. Two blocks from the stadium, we could walk at a normal pace. The boss let go of my arm.

'What happened in there?' she demanded, her voice suddenly angry. 'One minute I'm talking to you on the phone, then someone else comes on the line and we get disconnected. After that, it just rings and rings.'

I told her about my encounter with Prefect and his friend.

'You're quite the little Bruce Lee, aren't you?' laughed the boss.

She wouldn't have laughed if I'd told her what else happened. How I'd been chased down to the footy oval and met Franky Budd. And what I'd said to Franky Budd.

A shiver passed through me. She'd kill me if she knew. Literally. Thank goodness there was no TV back at the hide-out.

A small green car pulled in next to the kerb. It was

the kidnappers' hatchback, with Steve at the wheel. The boss pulled open the back door.

'Get in,' she said.

I shucked off the heavy backpack and tossed it into the hatchback ahead of me. For a second, I hesitated. Now was my chance to escape. There were people everywhere – a thousand witnesses if the boss tried to stop me. And why would she? The money was in the car.

But then I thought of Tommy, and got in.

As we drove away, I wondered if I'd just made the worst decision of my life.

19
CALL OF NATURE

The boss didn't make me keep my head down on the way back to the kidnappers' hide-out. I guess she no longer cared if I knew its location. They'd be gone by morning.

There wasn't much to see anyway. It was dark by the time we left Hobart. When the last suburbs were behind us, the boss asked me for the backpack. I passed it through the gap between the two front seats. The boss switched on the interior light and undid the broken zip.

'Would you take a look at this!' she said, lifting out a bundle of one-hundred-dollar notes and showing it to Steve. 'Have you ever seen such a beautiful sight?'

'Never,' laughed Steve.

The boss shouldn't have distracted him. He took his eyes off the road at exactly the wrong moment. We'd just come around a corner. There was something on the road. It looked like a load of black garbage bags had fallen off someone's trailer. But garbage bags don't move. And they don't have red shining eyes.

They were animals – Tasmanian devils.

'LOOK OUT!' I yelled.

Steve slammed on the brakes. I was thrown forward against the tug of my seatbelt. Rubber shrieked on bitumen as we hurtled towards the scrum of devils. There were at least six of them. They scattered in all directions, revealing the half-eaten carcass of a wallaby that must have been killed by a car.

Our car went skidding past, narrowly missing the dead wallaby. But it didn't miss all the devils.

Thump!

We slewed to a standstill about twenty metres further on. The car leaned sideways. Two wheels were in the road-side ditch. Steve tried to drive out, but the engine stalled. He tried again. Same result.

'Useless piece of junk!' he snarled, and banged the

steering wheel in frustration.

'Or useless driver?' asked the boss.

'What was I supposed to do – run over them?' Steve said angrily. 'Tassie devils are as solid as bricks. Hit them in a tinny little car like this, and who knows what damage you'll do.'

'More damage than running off the road?' the boss asked.

'I didn't see them until it was too late.'

'You should have been watching the road.'

'Who was it who shoved a pile of money in my face?'

While they argued, I clicked my door open and got out.

'Hey! Where do you think you're going?' the boss called after me.

'Just checking the one we hit.'

'Get back in the car,' she ordered.

I kept walking. The kidnappers might call her boss, but she wasn't *my* boss. I didn't think she'd shoot me for helping an injured animal.

The devil looked like it was beyond help. It didn't move as I approached. It lay next to the dead wallaby, a lifeless black mound about the size of a pillow. Dead, I thought. I bent to drag it off the road.

Behind me, Steve started the car again. The engine roared as he tried to drive out of the ditch. I heard the wheels spinning in soft mud, but the car wasn't going anywhere. It stalled.

In the sudden silence I heard another sound. Raspy breathing. The devil was alive! It wasn't moving, but it was alive. I crouched over it, wondering what to do. Tasmanian devils didn't get that name for nothing. They're nasty. They have really mean tempers, and for their size, they have the strongest jaws of any animal on earth. One bite and I could lose a hand. That's not an exaggeration. I once read a magazine article about a horse that died one night and got eaten by devils – all that was left next morning were four iron horseshoes.

'Promise not to bite me,' I said, trying to build up the courage to pick up the devil.

The problem was that it was dark – I couldn't really see what was going on. Was the motionless black creature unconscious, or was it just waiting for my hands to get within biting range?

Steve started the car again. I heard the gears clunk and the reverse lights came on. They were surprisingly bright. Now I could see the devil clearly. There wasn't any blood and none of its legs looked broken. Most importantly, its eyes were closed. It was unconscious. I took off my blazer and carefully wrapped it around the injured animal.

As I lifted the devil, I was suddenly dazzled by headlights. A car had come around the corner and was speeding towards me. I quickly stepped off the road. The car slowed down. They must have seen me standing next to the dead wallaby, and seen the hatchback in the ditch a little further on, and thought there'd been an accident.

Back in the other direction, Steve gunned the hatchback's engine and reversed out of the ditch. He kept his foot down, roaring along the side of the road towards me, still in reverse.

The two cars stopped at the same time. They were about fifteen metres apart, with me in the middle. I was blinded by the new car's headlights. A car door creaked open and someone started to get out.

'Is everything all right?' a man asked.

Another car door opened behind me. 'We're fine,' the boss said. 'My son was just answering a call of nature. Come on, darling, back in the car.'

Before I had time to consider my options, the boss was standing next to me. She gripped my elbow and led me back to the hatchback, shielding her eyes from the headlights with her other hand. The rear door was already open. I had no choice but to get in.

'Thanks for stopping,' the boss called back to the other car, giving them a friendly wave before she slid in next to Steve.

She stopped being friendly as soon as she'd closed her door. 'No more chances, Mr,' she warned me. 'Next time you play up, you'll wind up as dead as your little furry friend back there.'

I thought she meant the wallaby. But as we drove away, I realised she was talking about the Tassie devil. Like me, the boss had been blinded by the other car's headlights when it pulled up behind us. She hadn't seen the bundle wrapped in my arms.

Neither she nor Steve realised they now had an extra passenger on board.

20
PART OF THE GANG

The other kidnappers were expecting us. When we arrived at the sawmill, Peewee was waiting in the dark outside the kayak shed. He lifted the roller door and Steve drove straight in.

'How did it go?' Peewee asked, flashing a torch into the car as the boss and Steve climbed out.

The boss dragged the backpack out after her and set it on the floor.

'See for yourself,' she said, lifting the top open.

Peewee shone the torch into the pack and let out a low whistle. 'Is it all there?' he asked.

'We haven't counted it yet,' the boss said. 'But I don't

think they'd short-change us.'

Steve picked up one of the bundles and sniffed it. 'Smells like it's all here.'

The other two laughed.

They seemed to have forgotten about me. I sat in the car with the wrapped-up Tassie devil on my lap, trying to decide what to do. It was still unconscious. For a while I'd been worried it was going to die, but in the last half-hour there had been some good signs. Its breathing seemed steadier and it had started twitching its legs. And just before we reached Sawpit Road, the devil had made a low growly sound. Luckily the boss and Steve didn't notice. But now I had to decide what to do with it.

The most sensible thing would be to show the kid-nappers. Then hopefully they'd let me put it outside, where it would be free to run off into the forest when it woke up. But it might not wake up. It was midwinter and really cold outside. If the devil was going to recover, it needed to stay warm.

No way would the boss let me take a wild Tassie devil – even an unconscious one – into their hide-out. But it was already in the car, and the car was quite warm.

Carefully, I lowered the devil onto the floor behind the driver's seat and hid it under my blazer. Then I slid out of the car and softly closed the door.

Peewee shone the torch in my face. 'So you decided to come back,' he said.

'I didn't think I had a choice.'

'Don't tell me you didn't *want* to come back?' the boss said in a teasing voice. 'You're practically part of the gang now.'

All three of them laughed. They were in a good mood. I wanted them to stay that way, so I played along with their joke.

'*Aren't* I part of it?' I asked. 'I was kind of hoping to get a sixth share of the loot.'

Steve ruffled my hair. 'I like this kid. He's got a good sense of humour.'

'I wasn't joking,' I said.

That brought even more laughter. I joined in. But I wasn't laughing on the inside. All sorts of thoughts were running through my head, and none of them were the kind that makes you laugh. Top of the list was: Am I going to get out of this thing alive?

Next on the list was: How's Tommy?

I soon found out. I could hear him crying the moment we stepped out of the kayak shed.

'Sounds like Peewee wasn't the only one who missed you, Mr Mum,' the boss joked as we walked across to the sawmill.

This time I didn't join the others' laughter. I was thinking of Franky Budd. He must have contacted the police several hours ago.

How long before they arrived?

21
TOMMY'S REVENGE

I didn't get much sleep. Tommy woke up at least once every two hours, either for a feed or a nappy change. Or just to be held and rocked. The boss was right – he *had* missed me. Angelo didn't know much about looking after babies. I suspect he'd been trying to feed Tommy cold milk. And he'd only changed his nappy once. Useless kidnappers!

They were annoying, too. When Tommy wasn't keeping me awake, the kidnappers were. I was locked in the campervan again, but I could hear them outside. Talking and laughing and making plans about what they'd do with the money. I listened to them counting it. Even in bundles of ten thousand dollars, it takes a long time to get to two million.

Another thing kept me awake. My brain. It wouldn't shut down. Even in those rare quiet moments when neither Tommy nor the kidnappers were disturbing me, my brain was ticking over. What if Franky Budd *didn't* contact the police? What if he did, and the police thought I was just some smart kid playing a joke? What if the police couldn't find the sawmill? I should have told Franky about the Crowford Kayaking Club.

What if the police found the sawmill, but didn't arrive in time?

From what I'd overheard, I knew the kidnappers were planning to leave the sawmill first thing in the morning. But they'd said nothing about what they were going to do with Tommy. Or what their plans were for me. I had a very bad feeling about that. Tommy was no threat to them – he was just a baby. But I'd seen too much and I knew too much. I'd be able to identify any of the kidnappers if I saw them again. And I could give the police good descriptions. I must have fallen asleep finally, because I had a dream.

I'm back in the steep narrow valley, practising for the heats of the Devil's Run Skiing Championships. Suddenly I hear yelling. It's not Princess Monica. It's a man. I can't hear exactly what he's yelling, just a word here and there: WEAPONS . . . DOWN . . . GROUND! There are some crashing sounds, too. And the thump of boots running across an iron roof high above me. I look up. There's no roof, only sky. And a cable car. Its door bursts open and something tumbles out. A baby! Launching myself forward with a double pole push, I shoot down the slope to catch it. But just before the baby lands in my arms, it morphs into Peewee.

That's when I woke up. I was no longer on Devil's Mountain, I was back in the campervan. Lying in a sleeping bag in the cramped floor space. Someone was leaning over me. It was too dark to see who it was. I could hear shouting outside, loud men's voices.

'POLICE! DROP YOUR WEAPONS! GET DOWN ON THE GROUND!'

Peewee's voice was much softer. 'Where's the baby?' he hissed, prodding me with his pistol.

Tommy was in the sleeping bag with me. It was the best way to keep him warm.

'I'll get him,' I said, wriggling out of the sleeping bag a little so I could reach round behind me.

I was still half asleep, but I knew exactly what was going on. The police had arrived. They'd broken into the sawmill just before dawn to surprise the kidnappers while they were sleeping. But they hadn't caught Peewee. He must have heard them coming and sneaked into the campervan without being seen. Now he was trapped. It was only a matter of moments before the police found him. That's why he wanted Tommy. If he walked out of the campervan carrying the baby crown prince with a pistol pointed at him, the police would have to let him and the other kidnappers go.

But I reckoned it was time the kidnappers stopped using Tommy as a hostage. My hands found what I was feeling around for in the campervan's dark interior.

'Catch!' I said, and flung it in Peewee's face.

Sometimes you hear people say, 'He didn't know what hit him.' It wouldn't have been true this time. Peewee knew exactly what hit him.

One of Tommy's dirty nappies.

'Urghhhh!' he cried. His voice sounded muffled.

Peewee dropped the pistol and clawed at his filthy face with both hands.

Now he was an easy target. A hammer fist punch to the chest sent him smashing backwards through the flimsy door behind him.

He landed at the feet of a tall, black-clad figure armed with a Heckler and Koch submachine gun.

22
DID YOU SAY FOUR?

Sergeant Pringle of the SOG (Police Special Operations Group) asked me to remain in the campervan with Prince Thomas until the area was secure. He meant until all the kidnappers had been rounded up. Another officer stayed with us, keeping watch at the door. It was getting light outside. A new day and I was still alive. Even though the danger was all over, I found myself shaking.

'Are you okay, son?' the SOG officer asked.

I guess he could hear my teeth chattering. It was embarrassing. 'I'm fine,' I said.

'We'll get the medic to check you out.'

That was even more embarrassing.

'I really am okay,' I said.

The medic was dressed the same as the others – black overalls and matching black helmet, and a black jacket with POLICE written on the back in large white letters. But instead of a submachine gun, he carried a medical kit. He gave Tommy a thorough examination, then it was my turn.

'Been to the footy?' he asked as he checked over my black eye.

I realised I hadn't washed my face since the boss painted it brown and yellow. 'I went, but I didn't get to see much of the action.'

'That's a shame. It was a really good game.'

'Were you there?' I asked.

'I took my son along,' the medic said, listening to my heart. 'He goes to Hobart Grammar, too.'

I was still wearing the uniform. I quickly changed the subject. 'How's Tommy?'

'He's a bit dehydrated, but overall the little prince has come through the whole ordeal with flying colours. Someone's taken good care of him.'

'Mr Mum,' I said softly.

Five minutes after our medical check-up, a helicopter landed outside. Two air ambulance officers came bustling in. But they weren't interested in me. Strapping Tommy securely into a small stretcher pod, they whisked him away, flanked by four heavily armed SOG officers.

'Royal cargo,' Sergeant Pringle said, as we listened to the helicopter lift off. 'Unfortunately, the rest of us have to drive. Ever ridden in a Hummer, Sam?'

He finally let me out of the campervan. I noticed two large, rectangular holes in the sawmill's roof. Sergeant Pringle's men must have quietly removed sheets of iron and slid down ropes while the kidnappers were asleep.

But now it was all over. Except for an SOG officer standing guard at the door, and another guarding the backpack of ransom money, the building was deserted.

'Where is everyone?' I asked.

'On their way back to headquarters with the prisoners,' Sergeant Pringle said.

'You guys work fast!'

He nodded. 'We have to, in situations like this. So we can catch them off guard. Four armed suspects, and they didn't get time to fire off a single shot.'

I didn't remind him that he and his men hadn't exactly caught Peewee off guard – I'd been the one to do that. Something else he said had set my heart racing.

'Did you say four?' I asked.

Before the sergeant could answer, I heard the scuff of quick footsteps behind me. And felt something cold and hard pressed against the side of my head.

'Tell your men to drop their guns, Sergeant,' the boss said. 'Or the kid gets it.'

23
SCREECH!

The boss hadn't been asleep when the SOG launched their raid. She must have been visiting the toilet and heard all the shouting. She'd hidden in a pile of sawdust down the back of the building, staying there until the arrests had been made and nearly everyone had left. Then she'd made her move.

'Chauncy, Evans, put your weapons down,' Sergeant Pringle told the other two SOG officers. He lay his own submachine gun on the floor near his feet.

'Hands up, all three of you!' shouted the boss. Her voice sounded really loud in my ear. 'Walk away from your guns! Go and stand next to that big saw!'

When the three SOG officers were lined up next to the saw, the boss shifted her pistol from the side of my head to my back. She gave me a vicious prod.

'Get their handcuffs, Mr Mum. Lock them to the saw frame.'

The three officers stood as still as statues while I clicked one end of their handcuffs around their wrists, the other end to the rusty iron frame of the giant circular saw.

'Do them up nice and tight,' the boss said.

I had no choice but to obey her. I felt really bad.

'Now get the handcuff keys,' she ordered, 'and chuck them to me.'

When I turned around to toss her the keys, I saw that the boss had exchanged her pistol for Sergeant Pringle's submachine gun. She slipped the keys into her pocket, then waved the evil-looking weapon at me.

'Get the backpack, Mr Mum. We're going for a drive.'

She had a final message for Sergeant Pringle and his men before we left.

'If anyone tries to follow us, or if there are roadblocks, the kid gets it.'

We all knew she meant it.

The boss made me walk ahead of her, carrying the backpack filled with money. There was a big black Hummer parked outside the sawmill with POLICE written on its door. We walked past it. The boss didn't have to tell me where we were going. I made straight for the King Club.

There was a blood-curdling screech. It was the most horrific sound I'd ever heard – worse than anything in a horror movie. And it was even more horrific the second time. As we walked towards the shed, there was a series of screeches, each one louder and more chilling than the one before it.

'What *is* it?' gasped the boss.

My brain raced. 'It's just that lyrebird. They make all sorts of noises – not just chainsaws.'

'I think I liked its chainsaw imitation better,' the boss said.

She'd bought it. She believed me.

When we reached the shed, I hitched the backpack over one shoulder so I could open the roller door. As soon as the door slid up, the noise stopped. Just as I'd hoped.

The boss prodded me in the spine with the barrel of the submachine gun.

'Get into the car.'

As I walked around the passenger side of the hatch-back, I saw the devil staring out at me from the backseat. It looked fully recovered. Instead of retreating to the other end of the seat like a normal wild animal, it put its front paws on the window and opened its mouth in a silent snarl.

Tassie devils' mouths are huge. All I could see through the fogged-up glass was a big pink oval surrounded by teeth. The teeth were big and pointy and they looked razor sharp.

I reached for the door handle.

The boss was standing behind the car. A plastic sun protector on the outside of the rear window prevented her from seeing inside.

'Not in the back,' she told me. 'I want you in the front where I can keep an eye on you.'

'I'll just put the money in the back,' I said.

I clicked the handle only halfway up, pretending it wouldn't go any further.

'The door's locked,' I said.

The boss rolled her eyes. 'I told Steve no one was

going to steal a car around here!' she grumbled.

Switching the submachine gun from her right hand to her left, she fished the keys from her pocket and stepped forward to unlock the car door.

I kept my fingers on the handle until the boss was about to walk past me, then I tugged the rear door open.

24
DEVIL DANGER

You couldn't blame the Tassie devil for being mad at us. First we'd run over it, then we'd left it locked in the car all night. It had a score to settle. Flying out of the back-seat like a small black missile, it sank its teeth into the boss's left arm, just below the elbow.

It was the arm that held the submachine gun.

There was a deafening burst of gunfire – *Blam! Blam! Blam! Blam!* – and a row of nine-millimetre bullet holes ripped across the concrete floor, narrowly missing the boss's own foot.

The devil got such a fright it let go of her arm and went scuttling out through the roller door to freedom.

Everything had happened so quickly that the boss hadn't even had time to scream.

But she wasn't the screaming type. Gritting her teeth, she dropped the gun and fell against the side of the hatchback, clutching her injured arm.

I picked up the gun and pointed it at her. 'Sorry about your arm,' I said.

The boss turned her eyes on me. I've never seen such a scary look – from a human.

'You knew that animal was in the car, didn't you?'

'I put it there,' I said.

The boss nodded. 'I should have shot you the first time we met.'

'Then they'd be locking you up for murder, not just for kidnapping.'

'Nobody's locking me up,' she said.

Pushing herself upright, the boss picked up the back-pack, which I'd dropped on the floor when I let the Tassie devil out, and flung it onto the backseat. Then she slammed the door.

'What are you doing?' I asked.

'Leaving.'

I raised the gun to my shoulder. 'No you're not.'

She laughed. 'You're not going to shoot me, Mr Mum.'

She was right – I could never shoot someone. I watched the boss tie her scarf around her bleeding arm. Then she walked around the other side of the car and got in.

'So long,' she said, and reversed out of the shed.

I leaned the gun against a stack of kayaks and followed her out into the grey morning light. I felt tired and defeated, like you do when your footy team has lost the grand final. The boss had won.

Or had she?

The car stopped for about three seconds as the boss changed from reverse gear into first. That's when I made my move. I rushed over, yanked the passenger door open, and jumped in next to her. The car had just started moving.

'Hey!' yelled the boss. 'What do you think you're doing?'

I didn't say anything. There wasn't a plan in my head. I guess I just didn't want her to get away after everything she had done.

'Get out!' she yelled, trying to drive with one hand and shove me back out the open door with the other.

But I was sitting on her left – the same side as her

hurt arm – so it was easy to fend her off. I didn't fight too hard – I would never hit a woman – but when the boss elbowed me in the ribs for the third or fourth time, I grabbed her sore arm. It must have hurt. The boss screeched like a Tassie devil.

'Stop the car,' I said.

Instead of stopping, she planted her foot on the accelerator. The car shot towards the bridge. I let go of the boss's arm and grabbed the steering wheel instead, wrenching it sideways. The car veered to the left.

It was heading straight for the river!

'*STOP!*' I yelled.

The boss wasn't listening. She hit me again with her elbow and tugged the steering wheel in the other direction. The car started to turn, but it wasn't going to make it. I let go of the steering wheel, grabbed the handbrake and pulled it up as far as it would go.

There was the sound of skidding tyres and the car spun in a circle. It came to rest, rocking slightly, on the very edge of the steep river bank.

'*Get out of my sight!*' she said.

She shouldn't have said it. Because her side of the little

green hatchback was hanging over the river like one end of a see-saw. Only my weight was stopping it from tipping over the edge. I opened my door and stepped out.

The boss's eyes widened in fear. Almost in slow motion, the car tipped and skidded down over the edge.

Oops, I thought.

Luckily the car didn't fall all the way down to the river. It came to rest three metres below me, wedged between the bank and one of the sturdy wooden bridge pylons.

The driver's window slowly rolled open.

'Help me,' the boss commanded. 'I can't get out.'

I scrambled down the bank and looked in. The boss was right below me.

'Help me out.'

'I didn't hear the magic word,' I said.

The boss looked confused. 'What are you talking about?'

'The one you're supposed to use when you want some-one to do something.' I glared at her until she got it.

'*Please* help me,' she said in a small, pleading voice.

She was no longer the boss.

'First, give me the keys to the handcuffs,' I said. And I didn't say please.

25
DANGER MAGNET

I got kissed by Princess Monica. Prince Nicklaus shook my hand. And Tommy blew me a raspberry. We were in a luxury hotel room overlooking the Derwent River in Hobart.

My parents were there, too. So were my little brothers, Jordan and Harry – at least, the twins *had* been there, until Franky Budd turned up with a football signed by the entire Hawthorn football team, and the three of them went down to the car park to try it out.

'Your son is an outstanding young man,' Prince Nicklaus said to my parents.

'Thank you, Your Highness,' Mum and Dad said together.

'No, it is we who should be thanking you, Mr and Mrs

Fox,' said the prince. 'As they say in our country, the child is a reflection of their parents.'

'Thank you, Your Highness.'

'Thank you, Your Highness.'

'We can only hope that *our* son grows up to be such a fine young man as your Samuel.'

Mum and Dad did their thank you thing again.

Princess Monica was sitting in an armchair holding Tommy. She winked at me. 'And so handsome, too,' she said. 'Even with a black eye.'

I felt the rest of my face turn red. And wished I was outside kicking the football.

Until Prince Nicklaus said, 'I have spoken to my father, the King, and he has offered your son a reward for saving his grandson.'

'I'm sure Sam doesn't want a reward,' Dad said.

Shut up, Dad! I thought.

'It really isn't necessary,' said Mum.

Shut up, Mum!

Prince Nicklaus held up his hand. 'My father insists, Mr and Mrs Fox. After all, Thomas is his only grandchild, and it is the King's right to give gifts when they are deserved. And in this case they are certainly deserved.'

The prince left the room and returned carrying a long, thin package wrapped in gold paper.

'The gift comes in two parts, Samuel,' he said, handing me the package. 'This part is from Princess Monica and me.'

The foil wrapping looked like it was made of gold. I tried not to rip it. Inside was a pair of slalom skis. They were Mattahorns, the kind used by the current World and Olympic champion. They must have cost a mint.

'Cool!' I said. 'Thanks heaps, guys!'

'*Sam!*' Mum hissed under her breath. 'They're not guys, they're Prince and Princess.'

'It's okay,' laughed Princess Monica. 'I was brought up in Australia. I kind of miss being one of the guys.'

Prince Nicklaus was smiling, too. 'Would you like to know about the second part of your reward, Samuel?'

'You bet.'

'*Sam!*' hissed Mum.

'Yes thanks, Prince Nicklaus,' I said politely.

He looked serious now. 'Unfortunately, Samuel, because our son was kidnapped, you and I were not able to ski together in the Devil's Run Championships. So my father has asked if you would like to come on holiday with the Royal Family to our mountain chalet next January.'

'But there's no snow in January,' I said.

The prince's eyes sparkled. 'There is in the Swiss Alps.'

'Wow! Cool!' I said. And turned to my parents. 'Can I go?'

Mum seemed doubtful. 'The Swiss Alps – don't they have avalanches?'

They have avalanches in Australia, but I hadn't told my parents. They worry about stuff like that. 'I'll be with Prince Nicklaus.'

'And with me,' Princess Monica said.

Dad said to Mum: 'I suppose if he's with the Royal Family . . .'

'. . . there won't be any danger,' Mum finished the sentence for him.

Prince Nicklaus was right – they were good parents. But they were good at forgetting things, too. A few months earlier, my big brother Nathan had called me a danger magnet, and it seemed to be true.

So I'd be in danger even if I *didn't* go to the Swiss Alps.

'Did you know you can ski down an avalanche?' I said, just to see Mum and Dad's reaction.